JESS KEATING

BUNBUN & BONBON

CAPTAIN BUN & SUPER BONBON

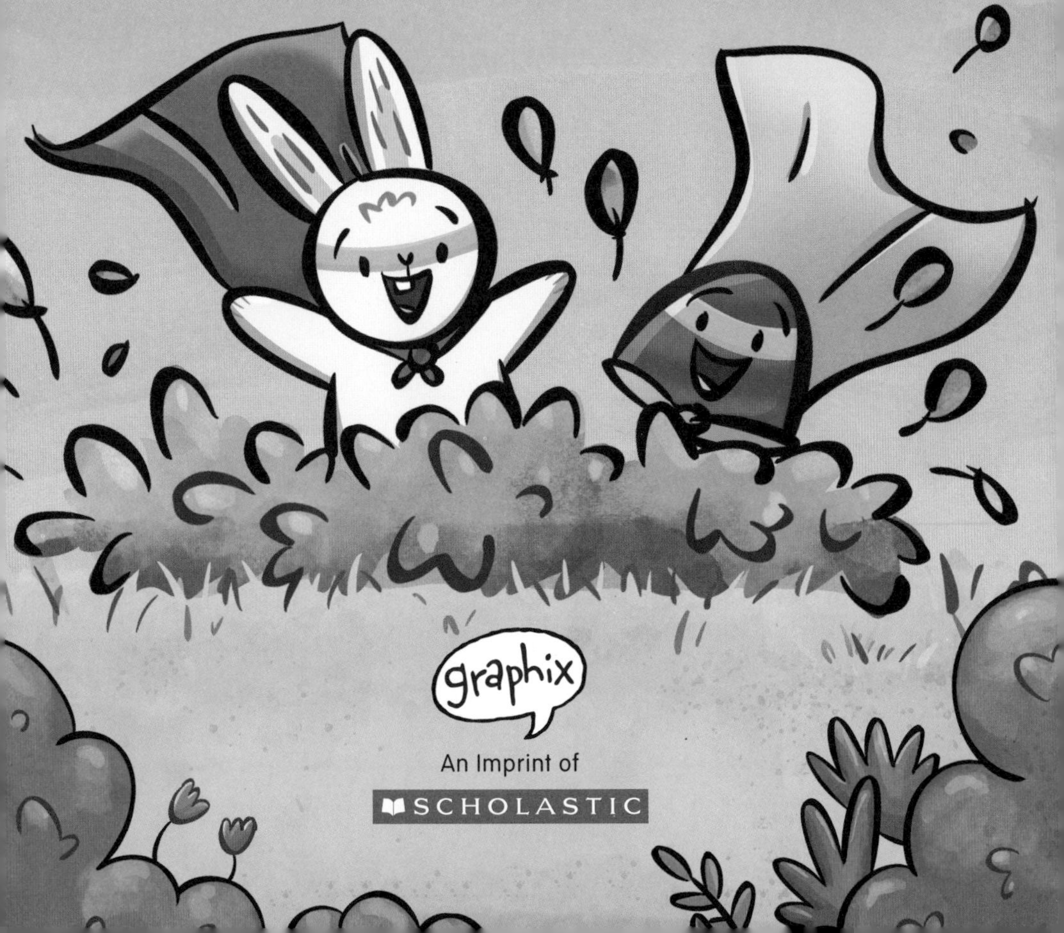

graphix
An Imprint of
SCHOLASTIC

To everyone brave enough
to share their superpowers . . .

Library of Congress Control Number: 2020950063

ISBN 978-1-338-74593-1 (hardcover)
ISBN 978-1-338-74592-4 (paperback)

10 9 8 7 6 5 4 3 2 1   21 22 23 24 25

Printed in China   62
First edition, September 2021
Edited by Jonah Newman
Book design by Phil Falco and Steve Ponzo
Color assistance: Wes Dzioba
Creative Director: Phil Falco
Publisher: David Saylor

CONTENTS

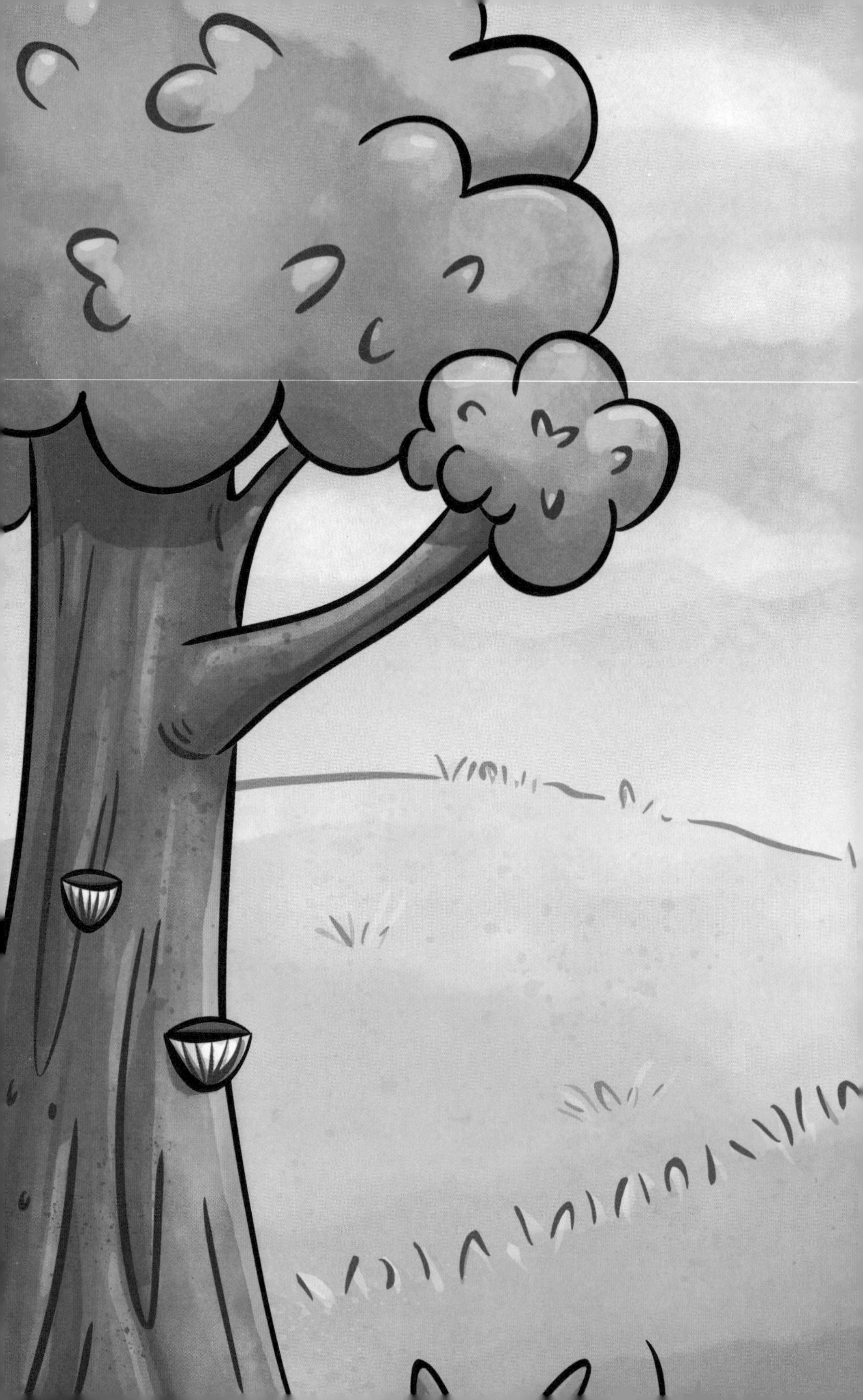

THE PERFECT DAY

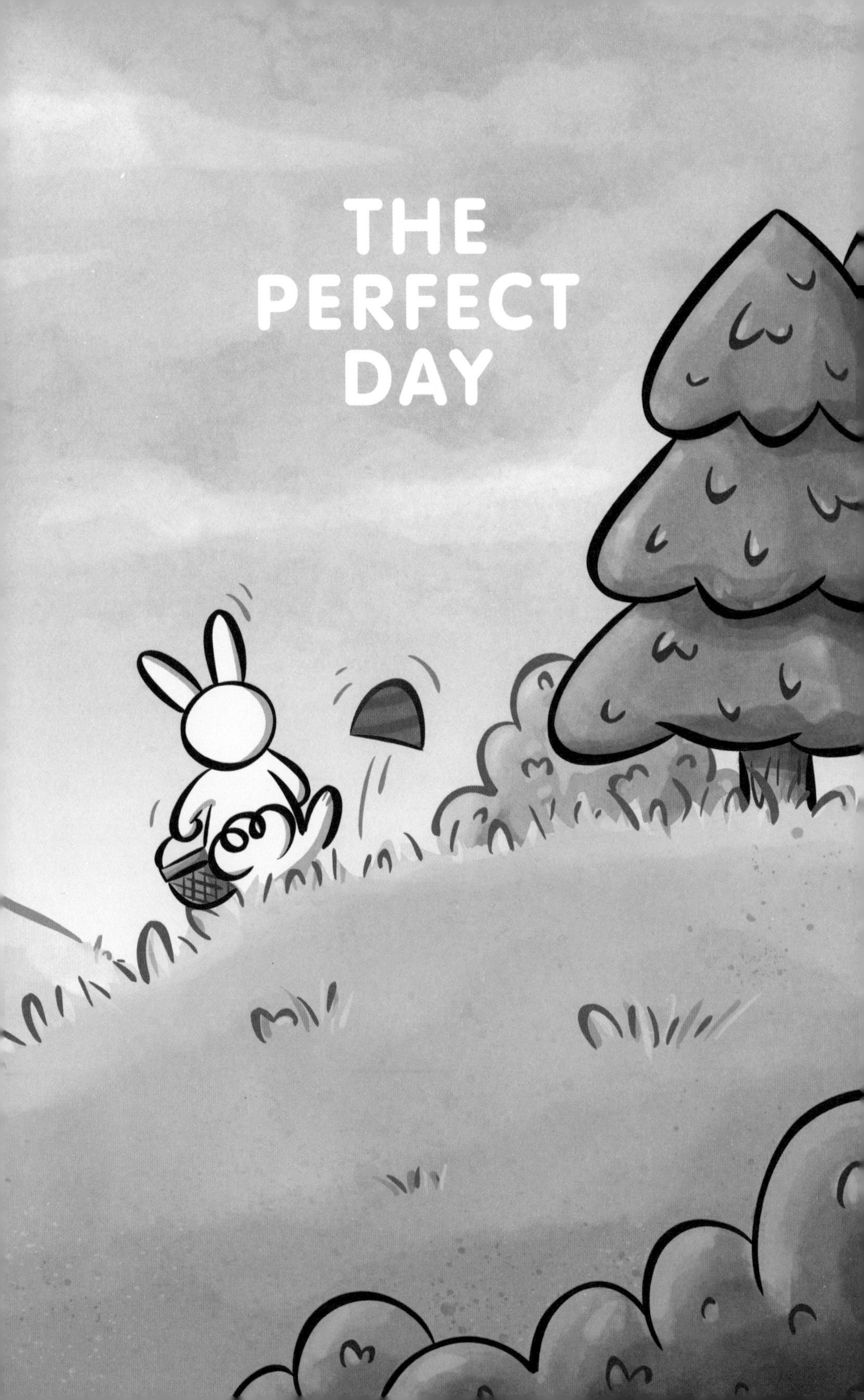

It was the
perfect day.

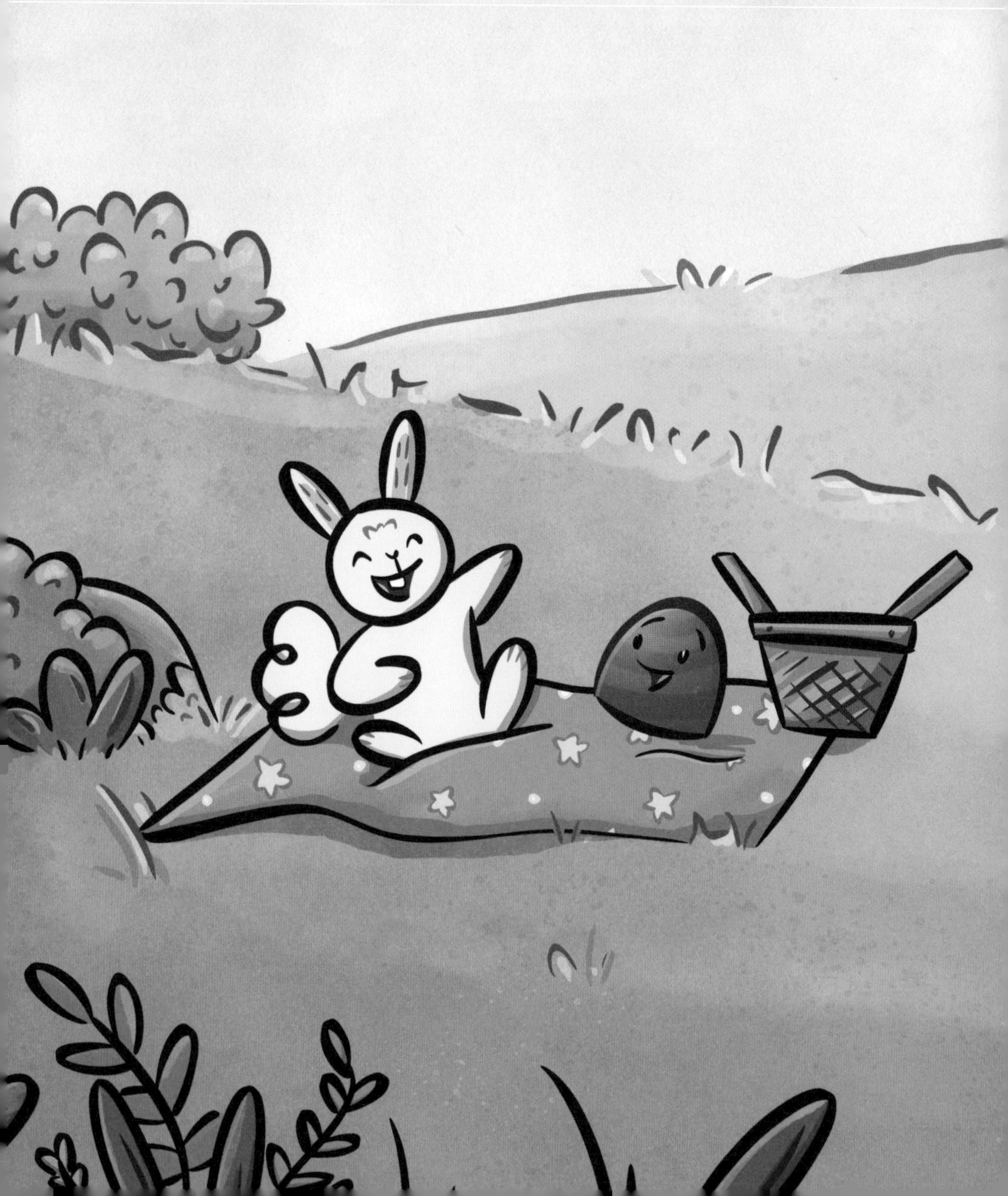

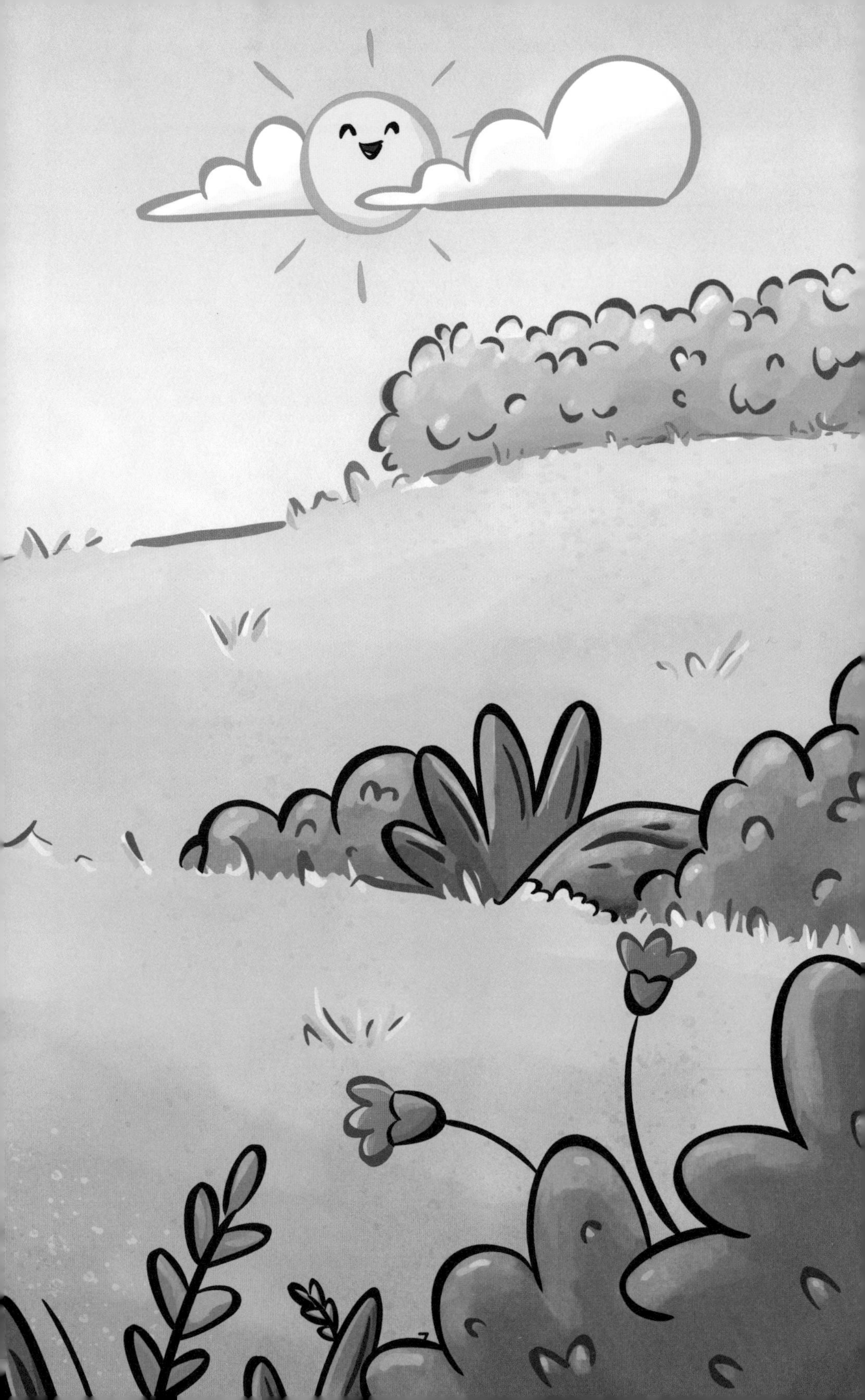

Bunbun and **Bonbon**
were having a picnic.

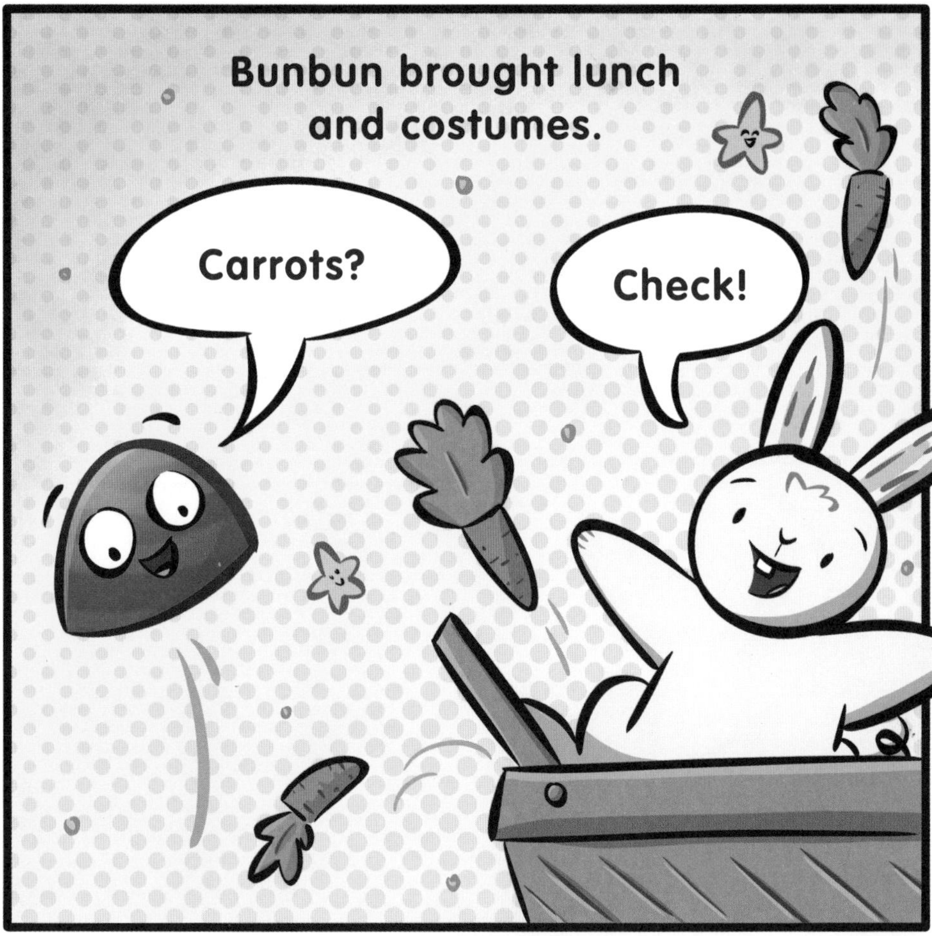
Bunbun brought lunch and costumes.
Carrots?
Check!

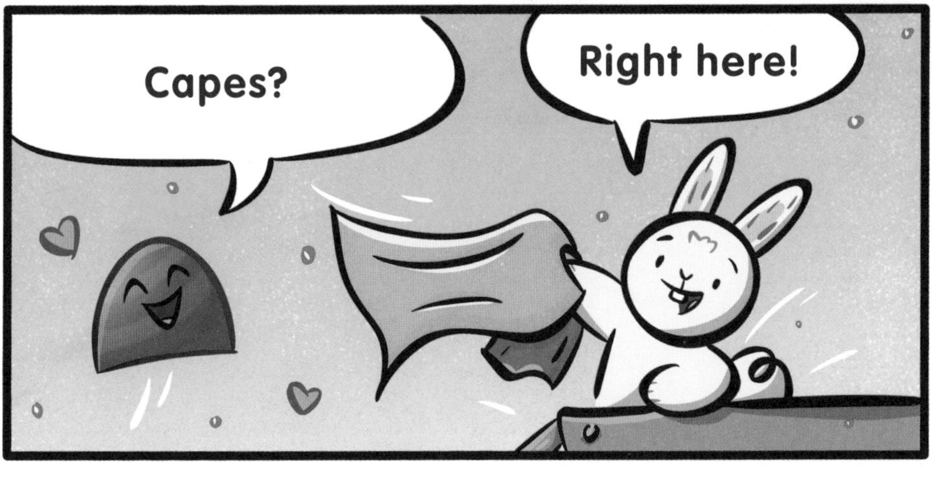
Capes?
Right here!

BONBON BROUGHT COMICS.

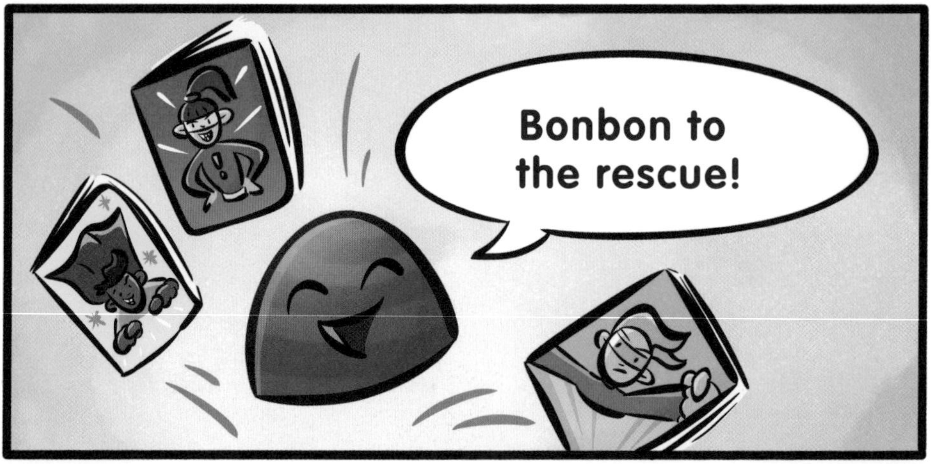
Bonbon to the rescue!

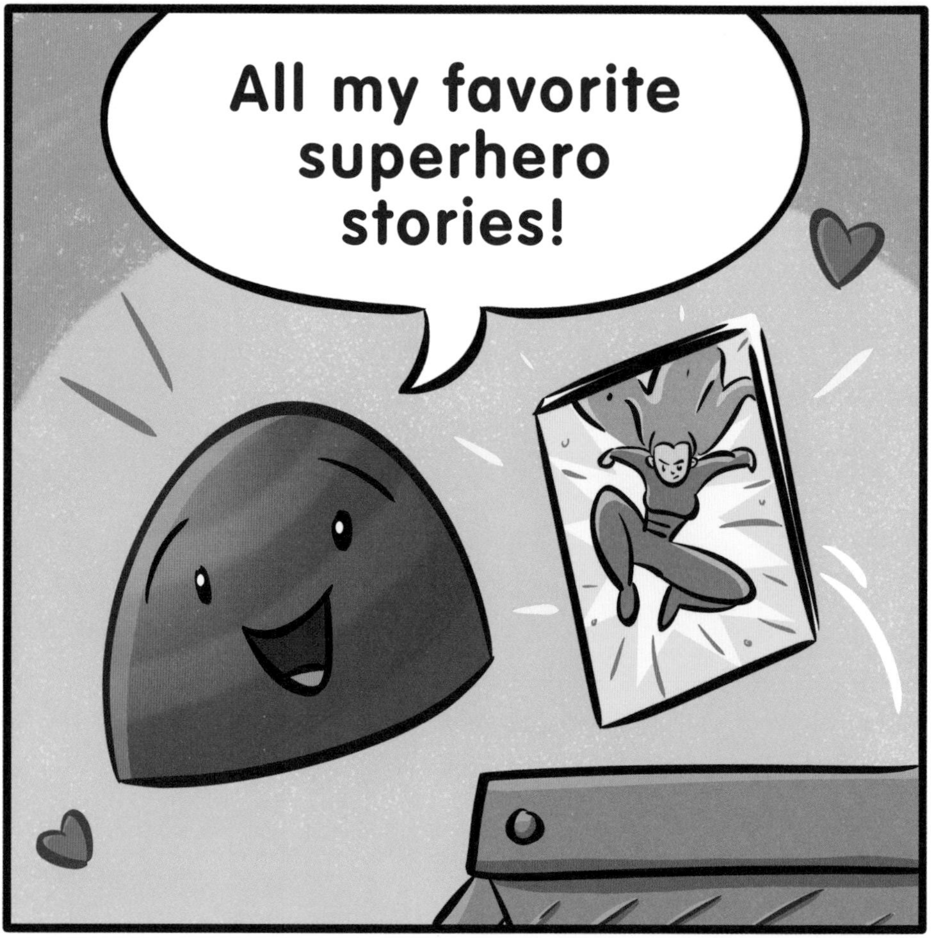
All my favorite superhero stories!

AND BONBON BROUGHT DESSERT.

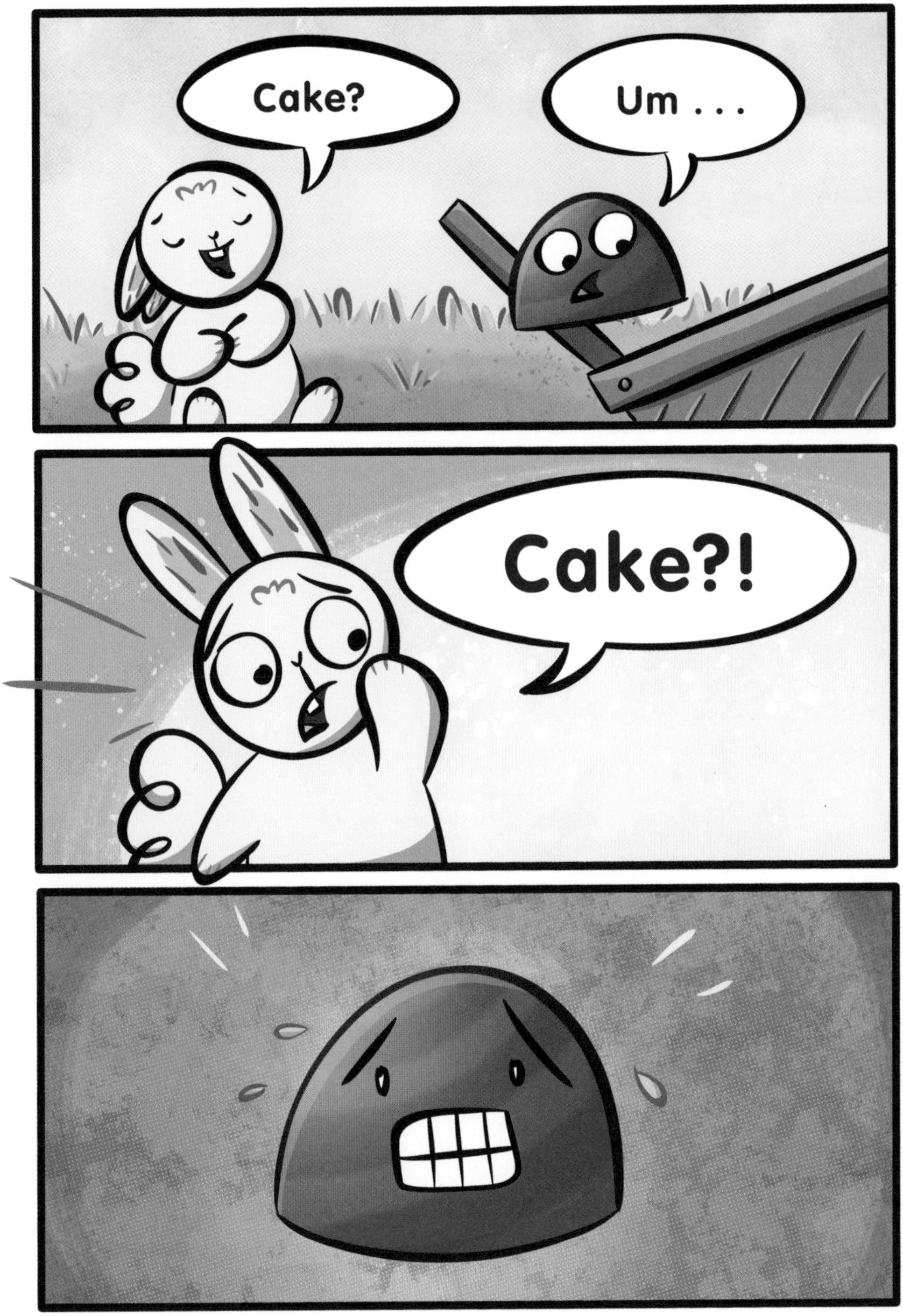
Cake?
Um . . .
Cake?!

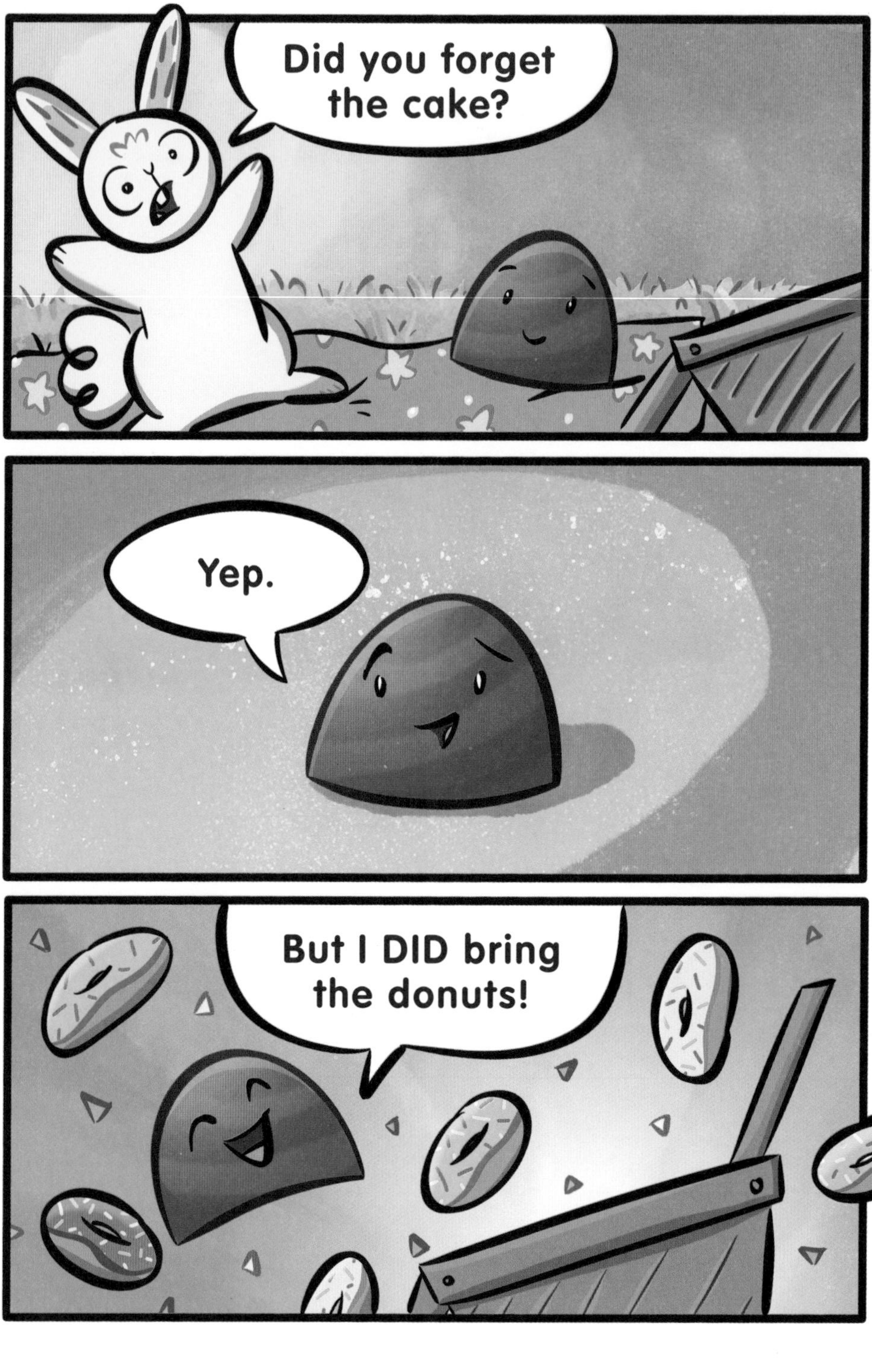
Did you forget the cake?
Yep.
But I DID bring the donuts!

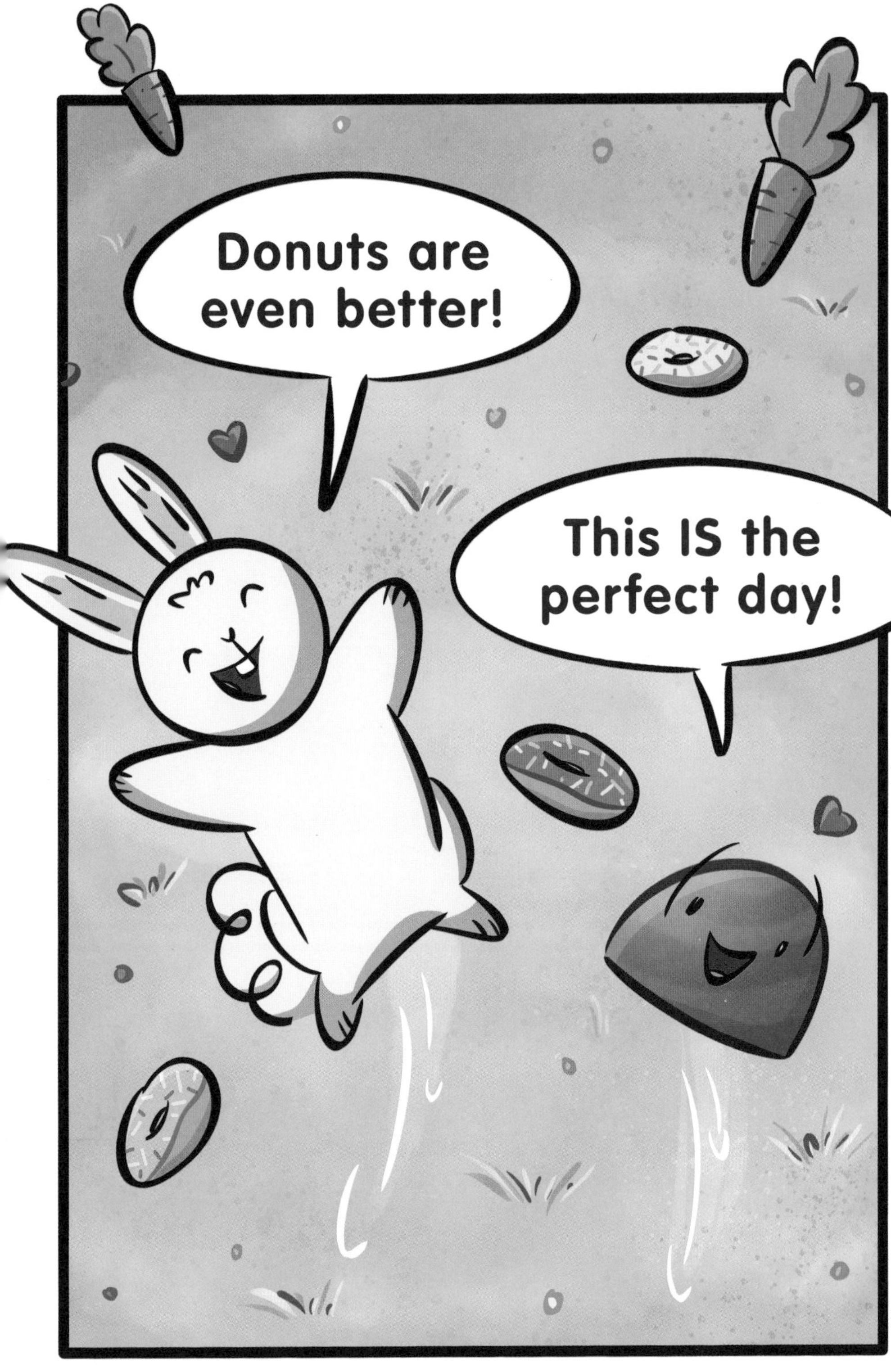
Donuts are even better!
This IS the perfect day!

IT WAS THE PERFECT DAY.

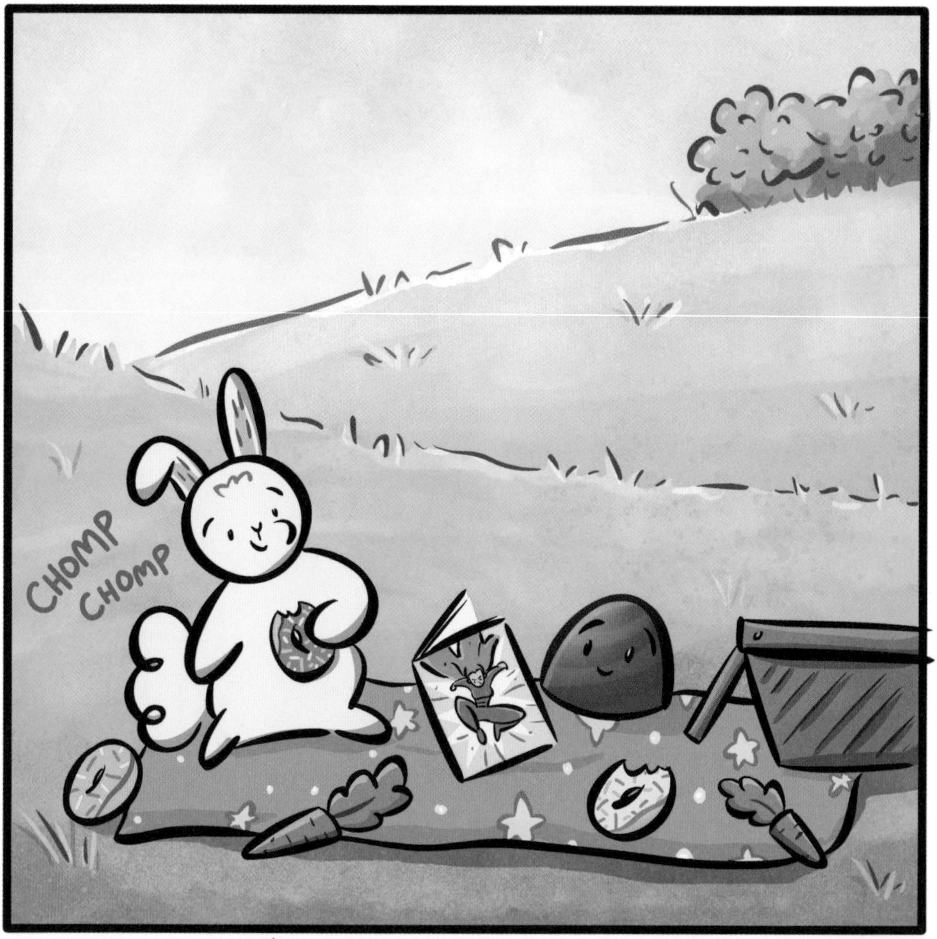
CHOMP
CHOMP

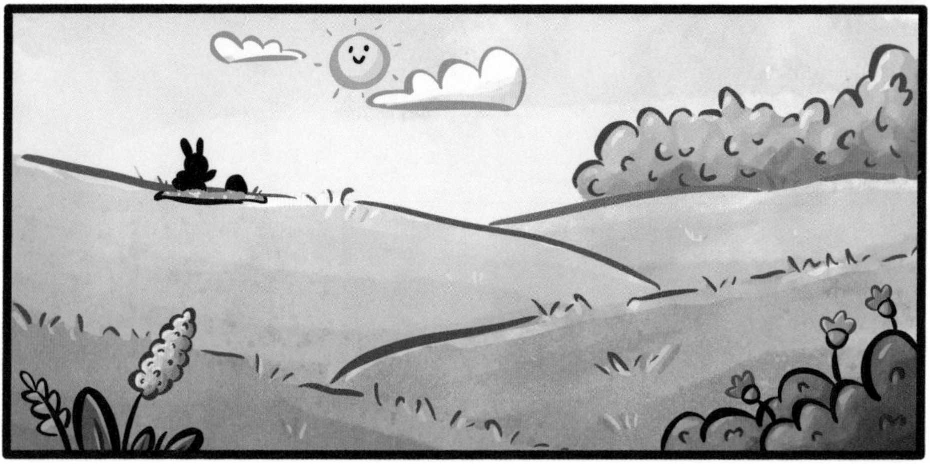

UNTIL . . .

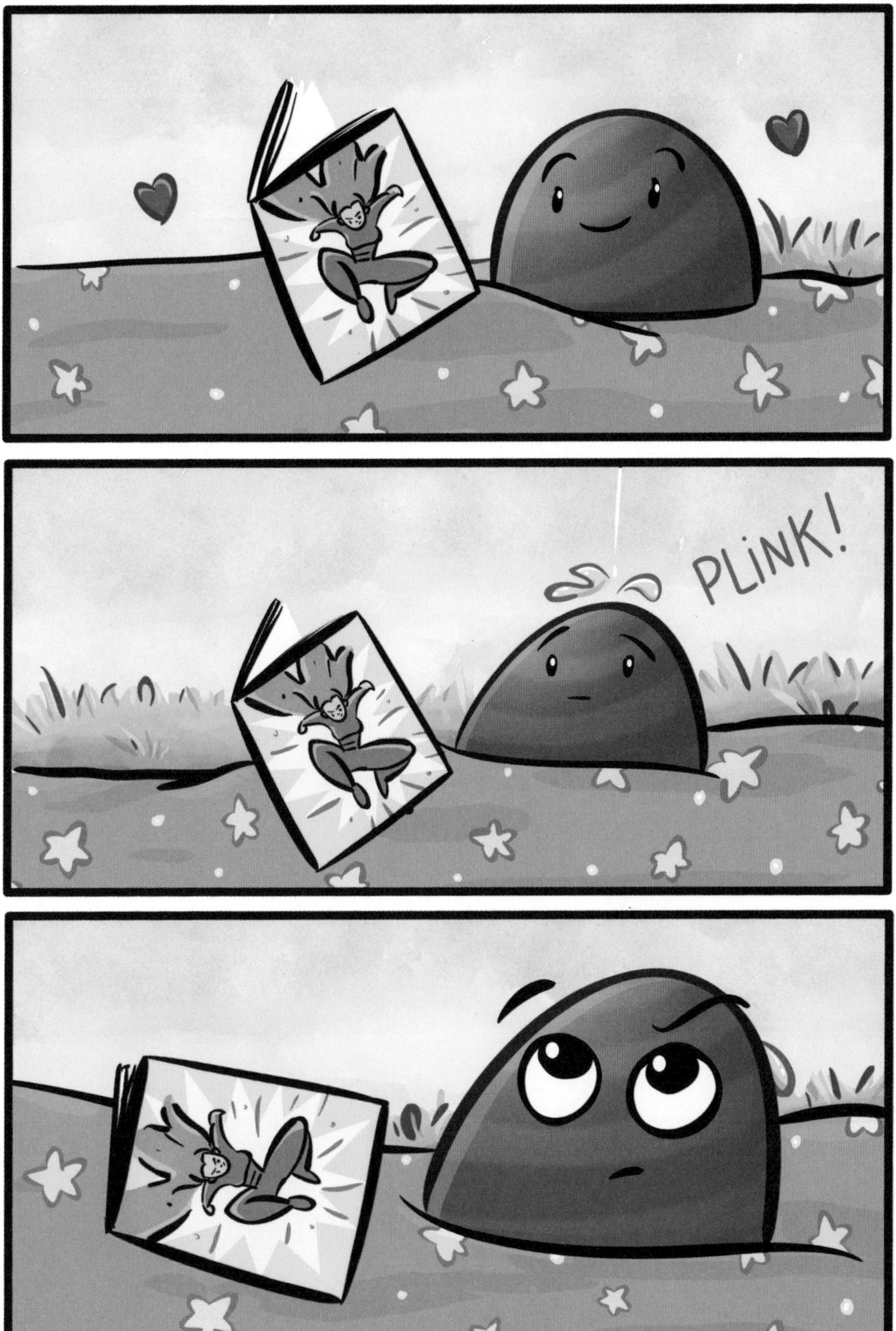
PLINK!

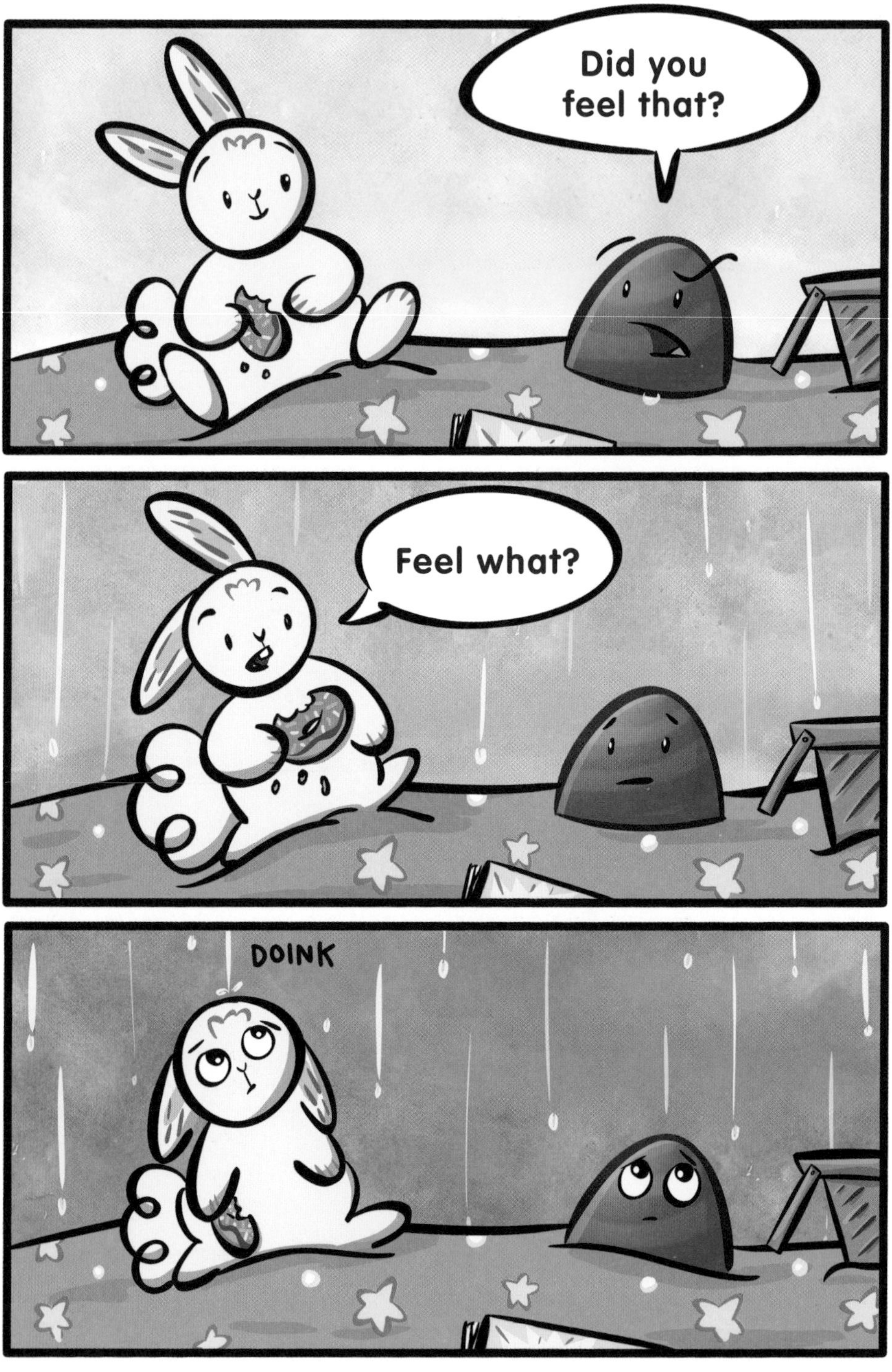
Did you feel that?
Feel what?
DOINK

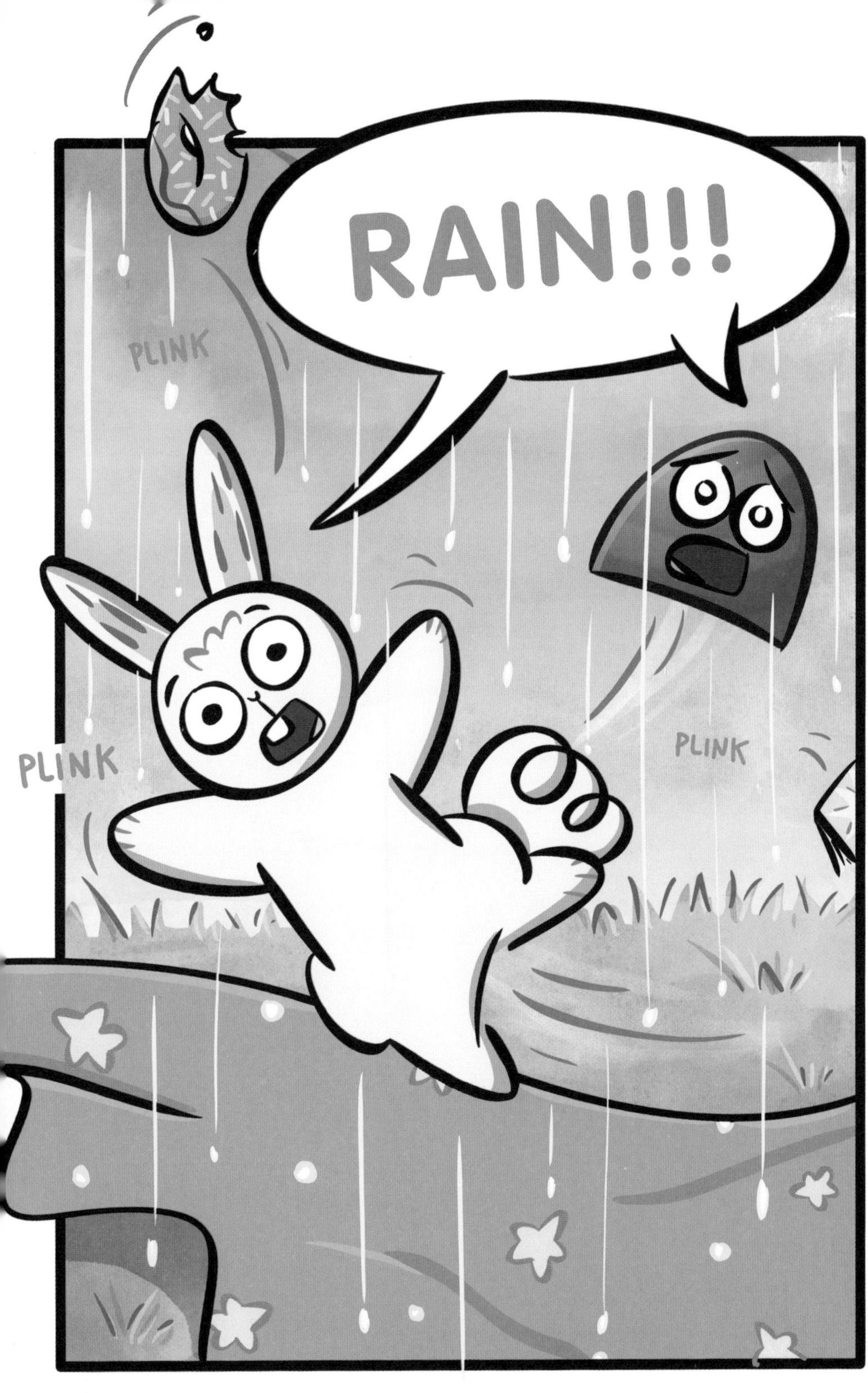
RAIN!!!
PLINK
PLINK
PLINK

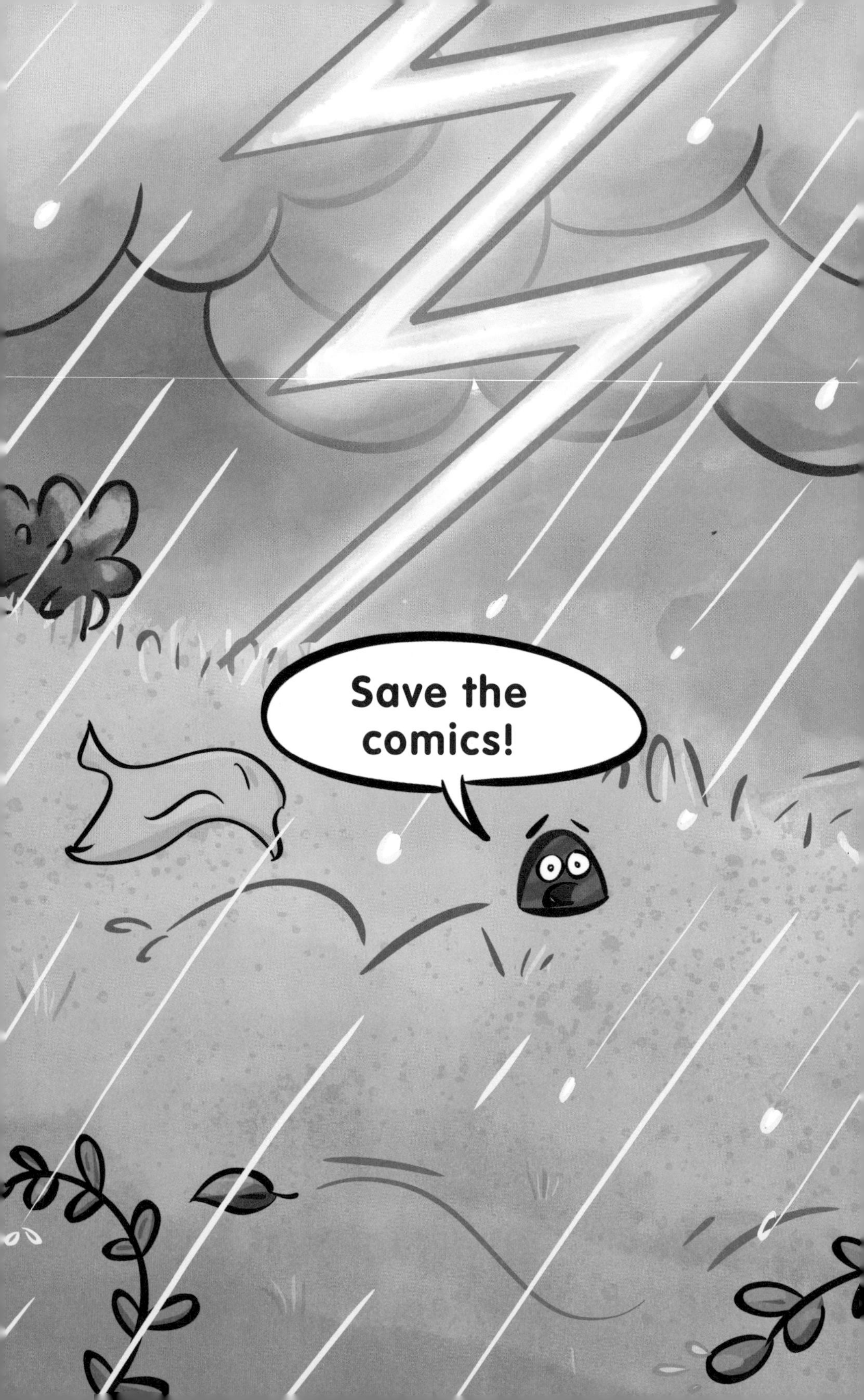
Save the comics!

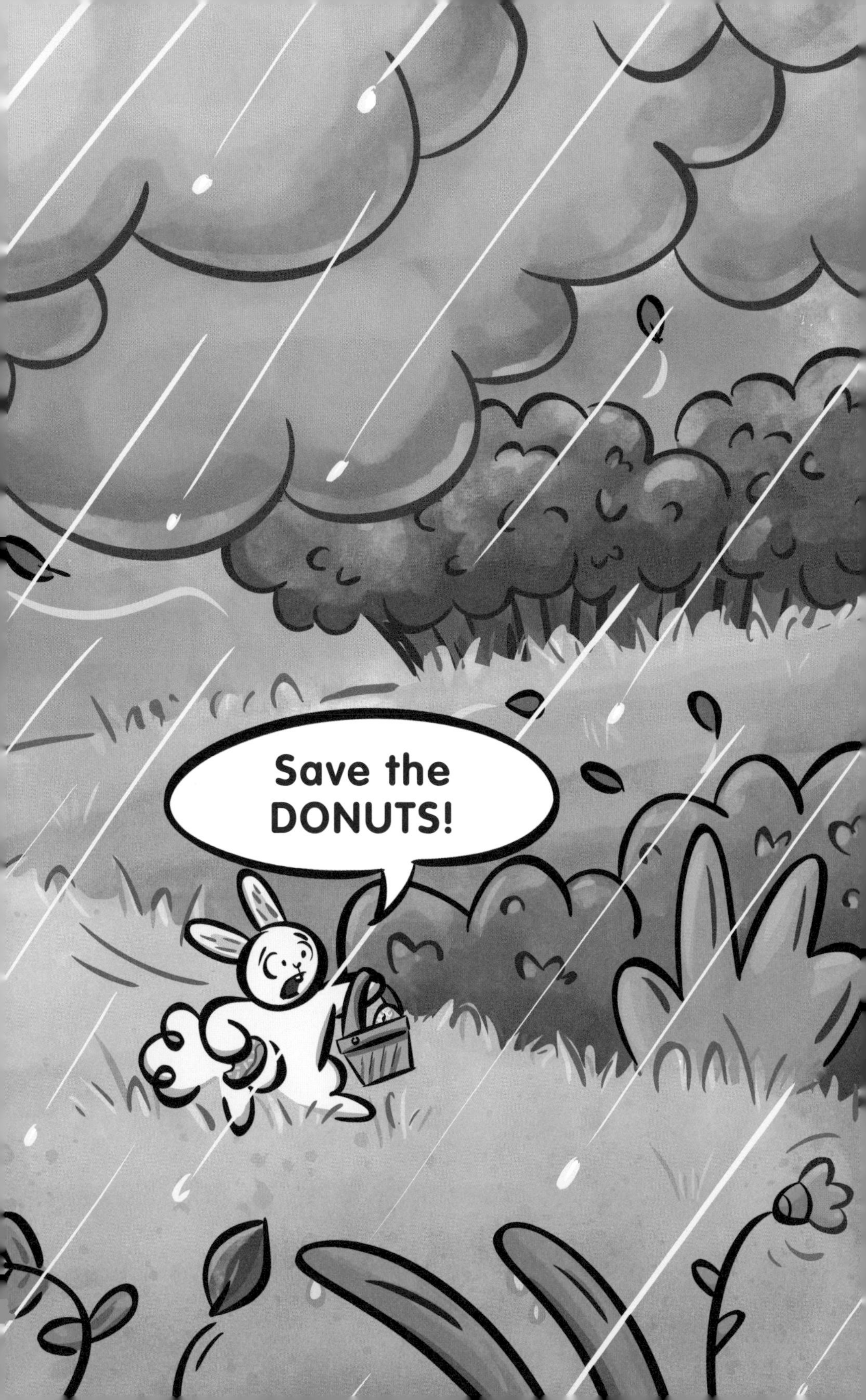
Save the DONUTS!

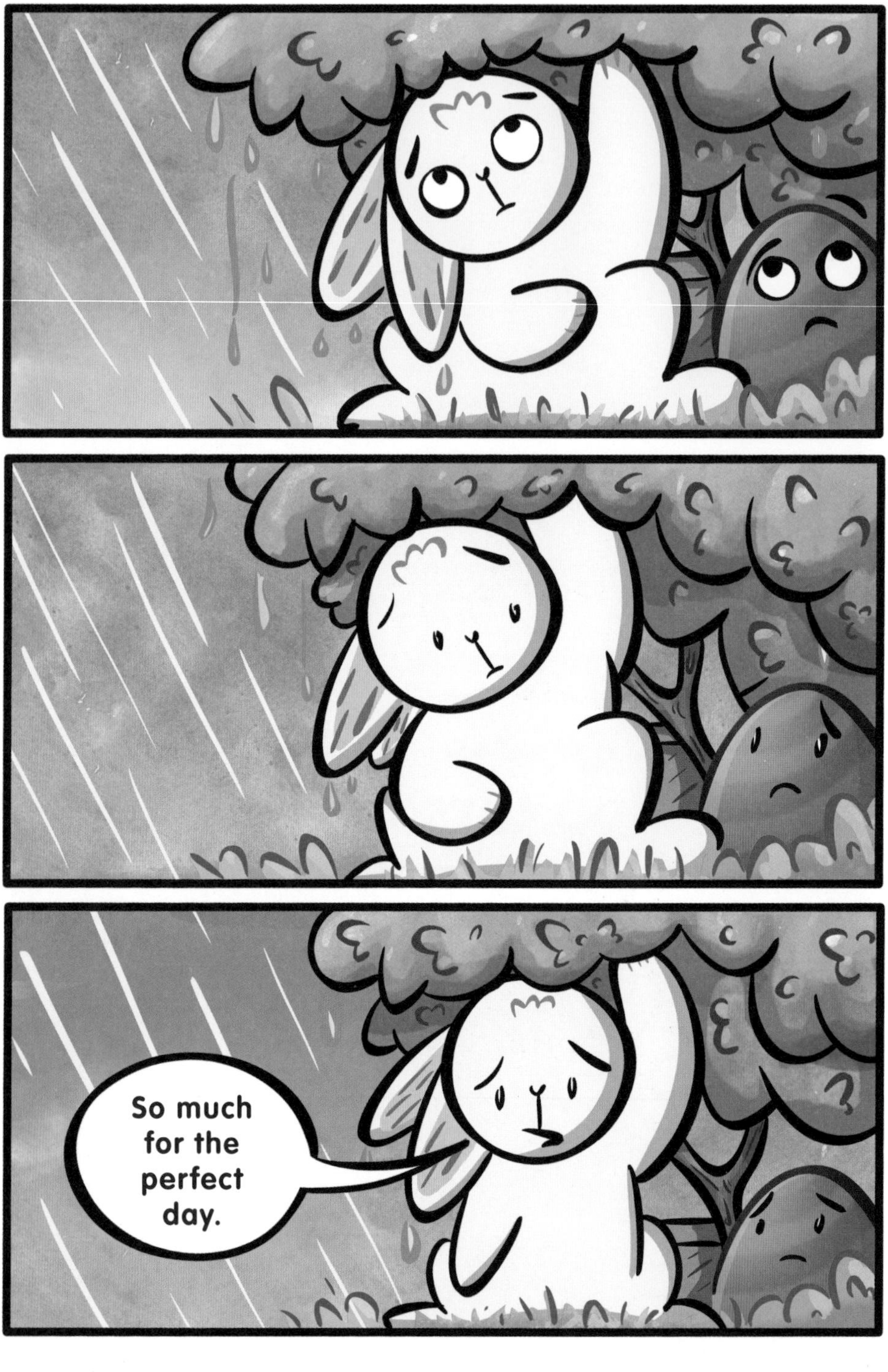
So much for the perfect day.

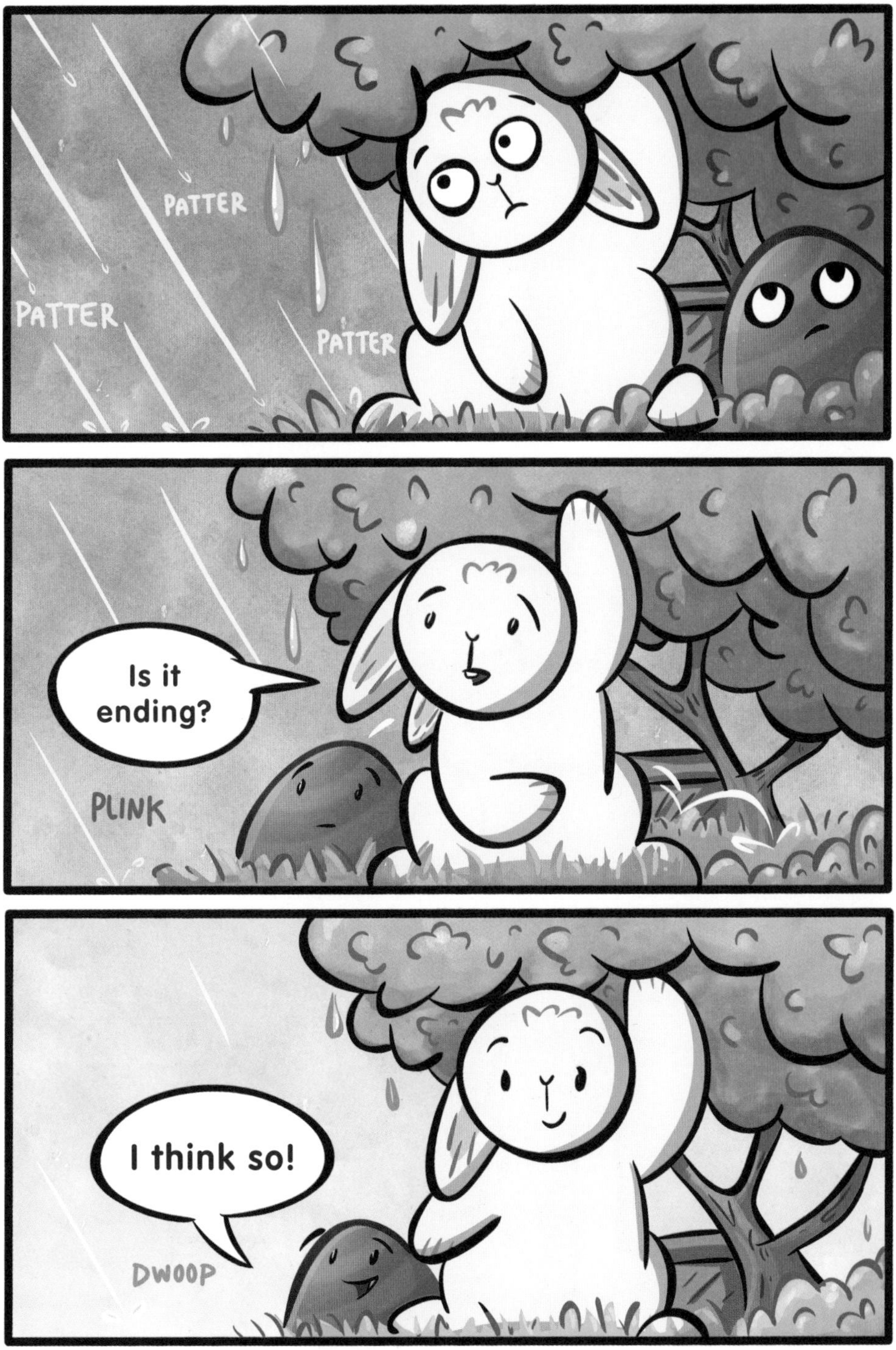
PATTER
PATTER
PATTER
Is it ending?
PLINK
I think so!
DWOOP

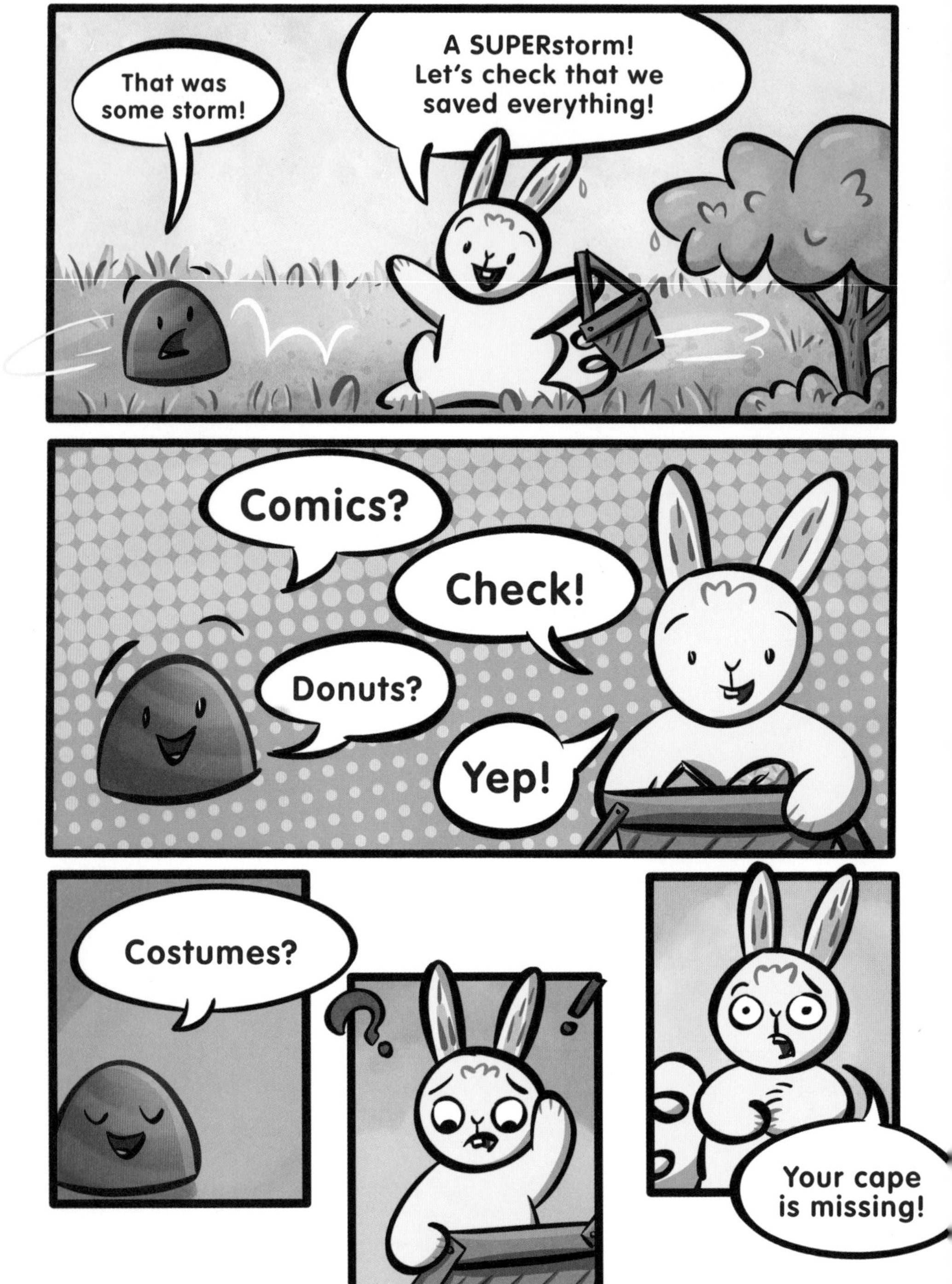
That was some storm!
A SUPERstorm! Let's check that we saved everything!
Comics?
Check!
Donuts?
Yep!
Costumes?
Your cape is missing!

AND SO . . .

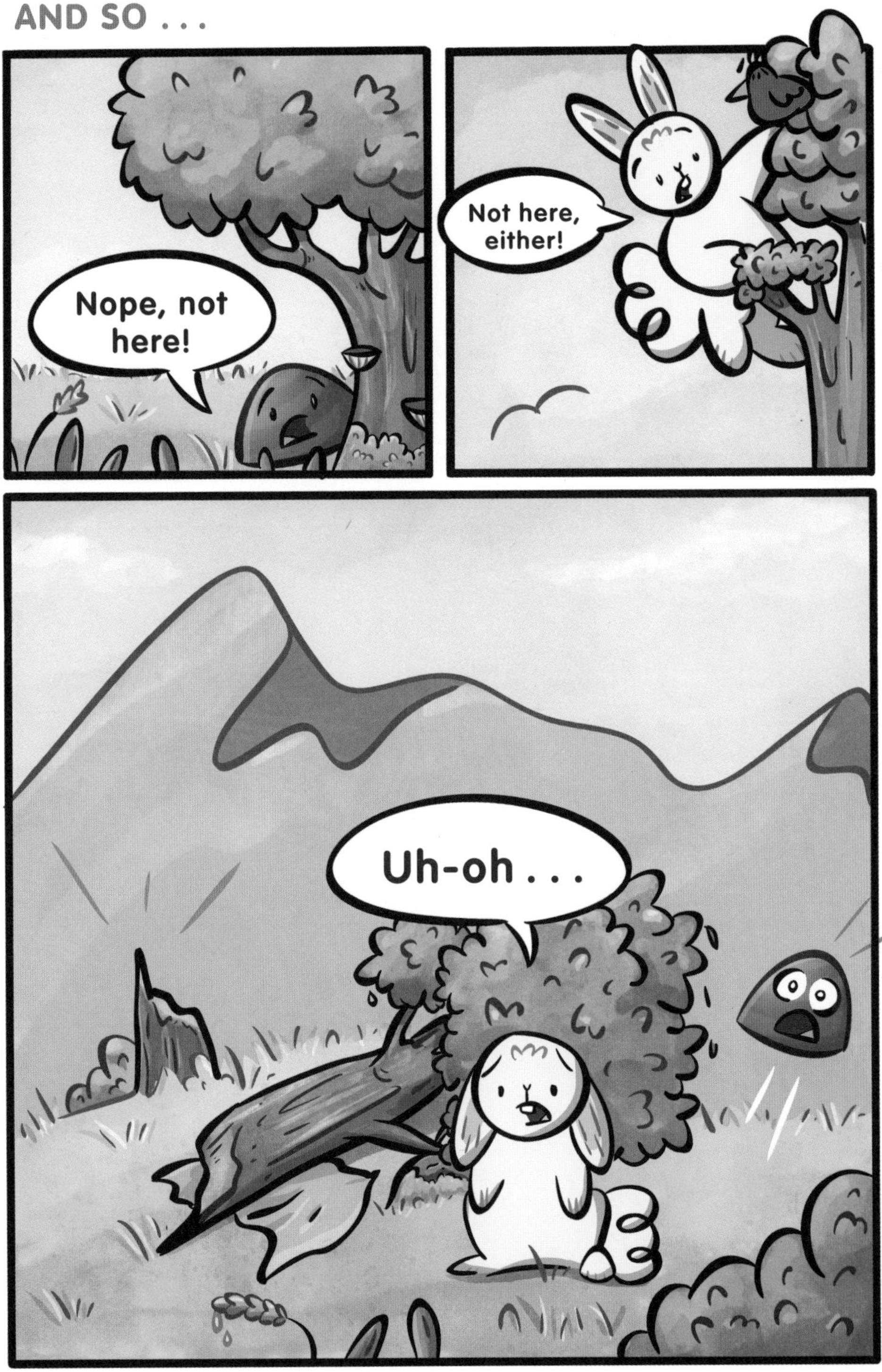
Nope, not here!
Not here, either!
Uh-oh . . .

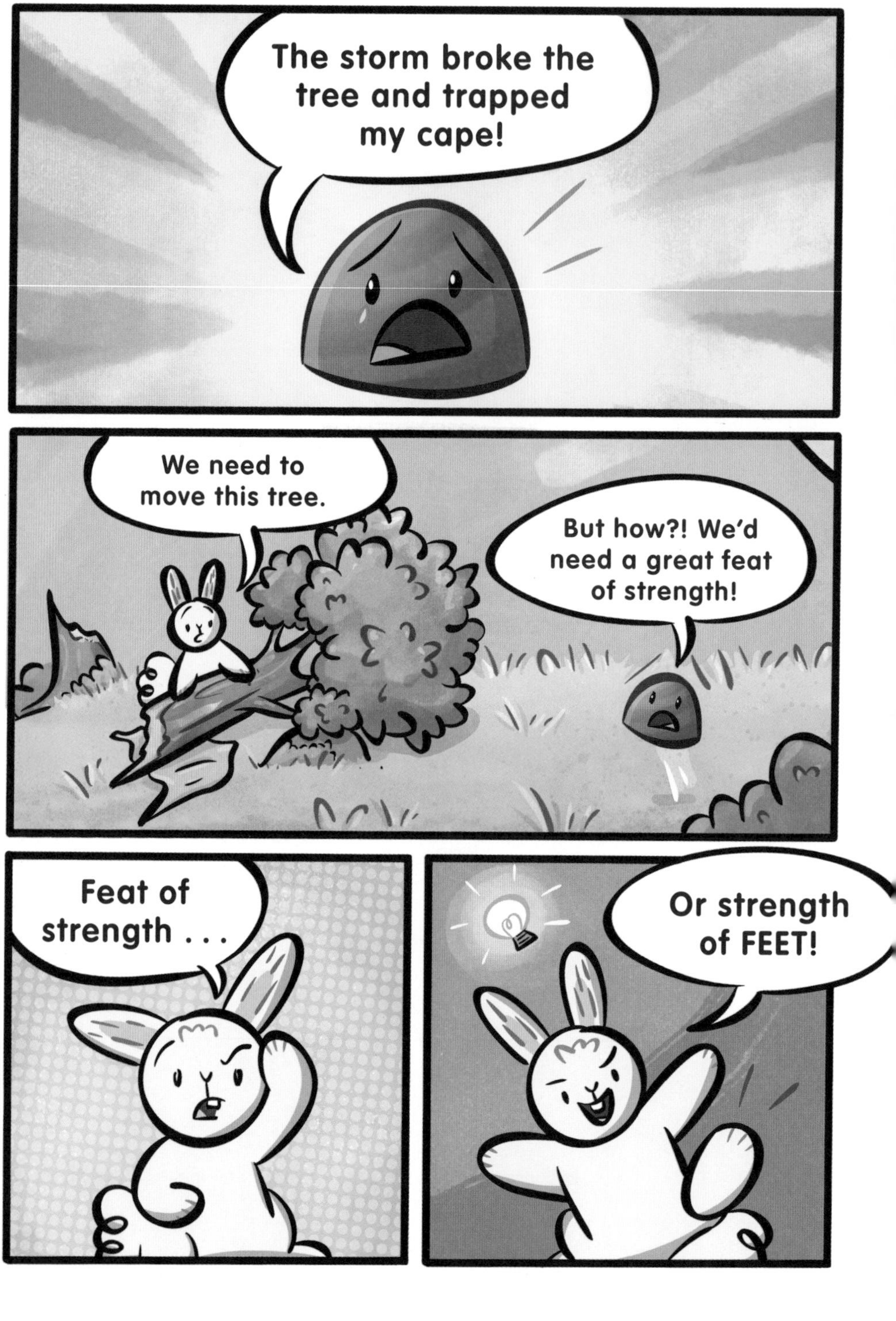
The storm broke the tree and trapped my cape!
We need to move this tree.
But how?! We'd need a great feat of strength!
Feat of strength . . .
Or strength of FEET!

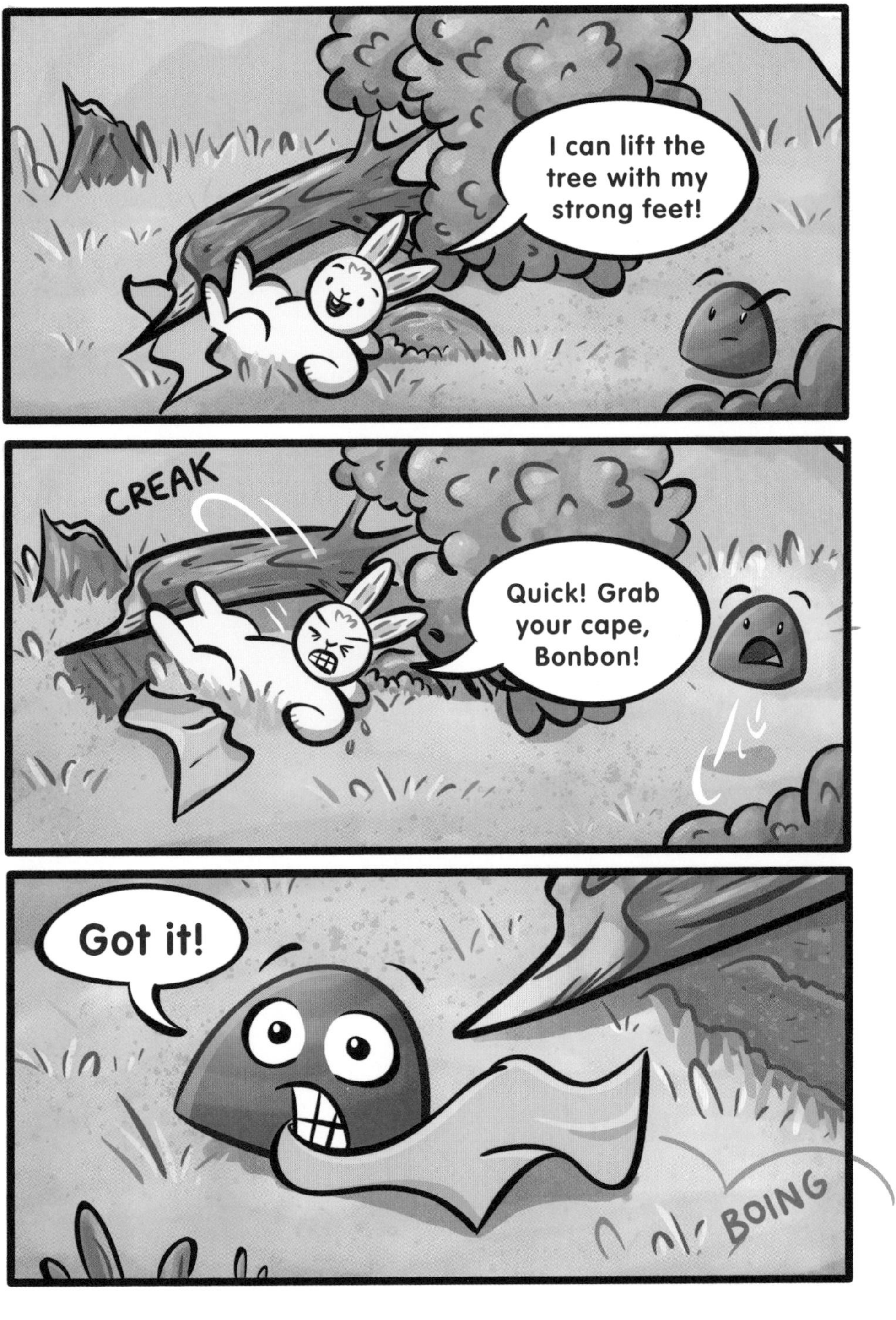
I can lift the tree with my strong feet!
CREAK
Quick! Grab your cape, Bonbon!
Got it!
BOING

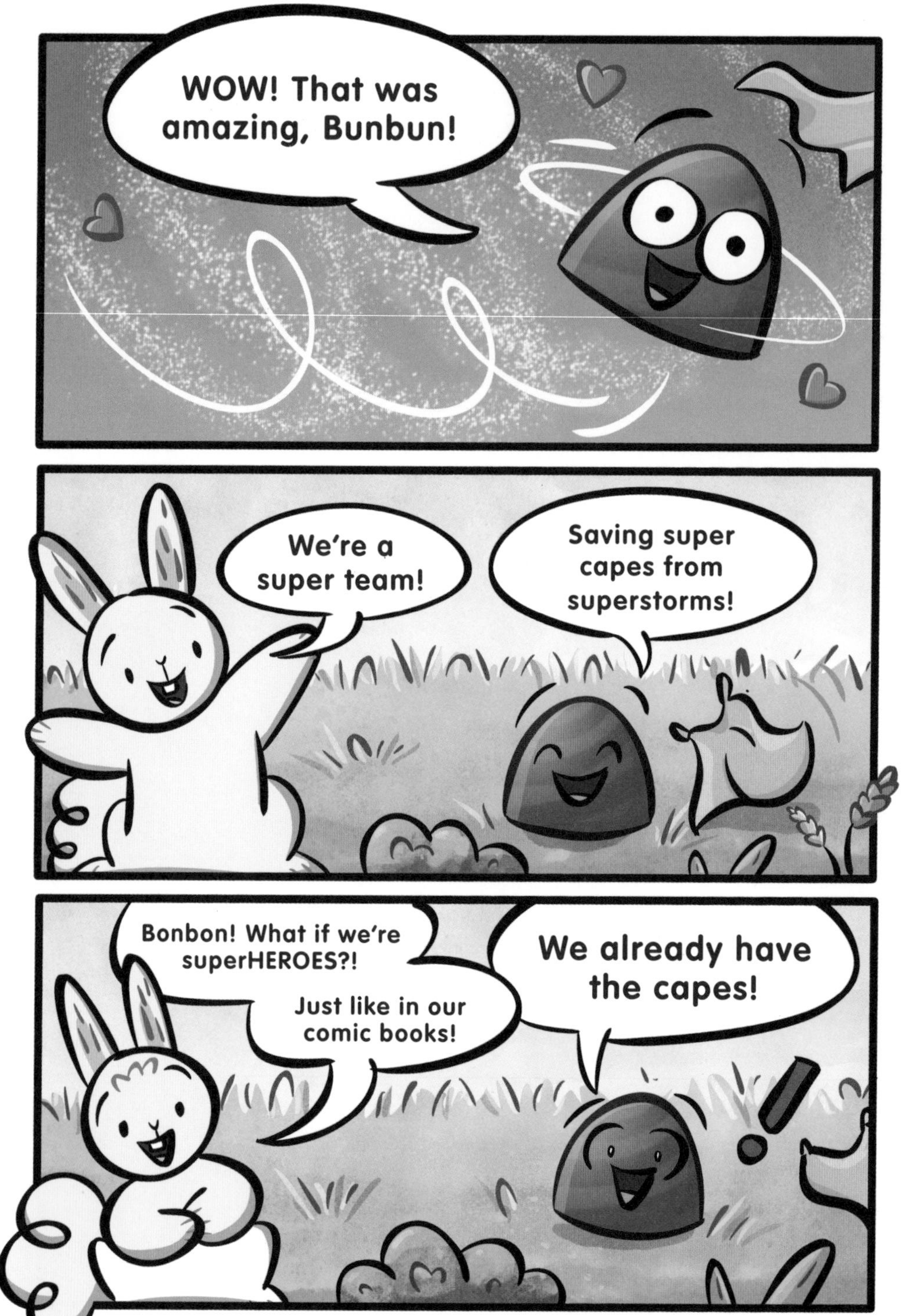
WOW! That was amazing, Bunbun!
We're a super team!
Saving super capes from superstorms!
Bonbon! What if we're superHEROES?!
Just like in our comic books!
We already have the capes!

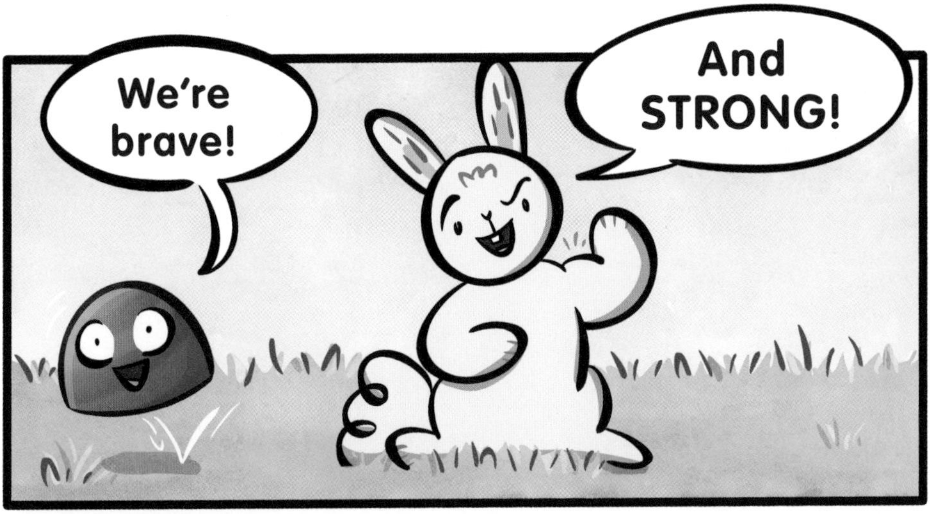
We're brave!
And STRONG!

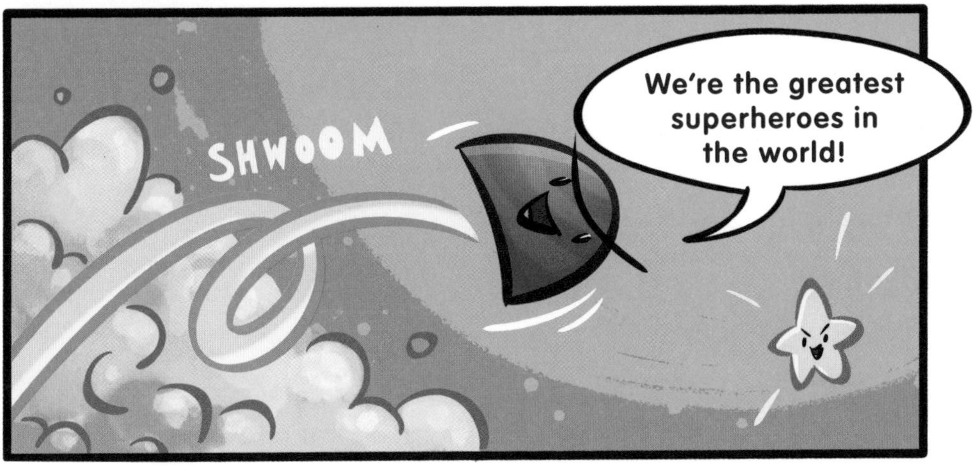
SHWOOM
We're the greatest superheroes in the world!

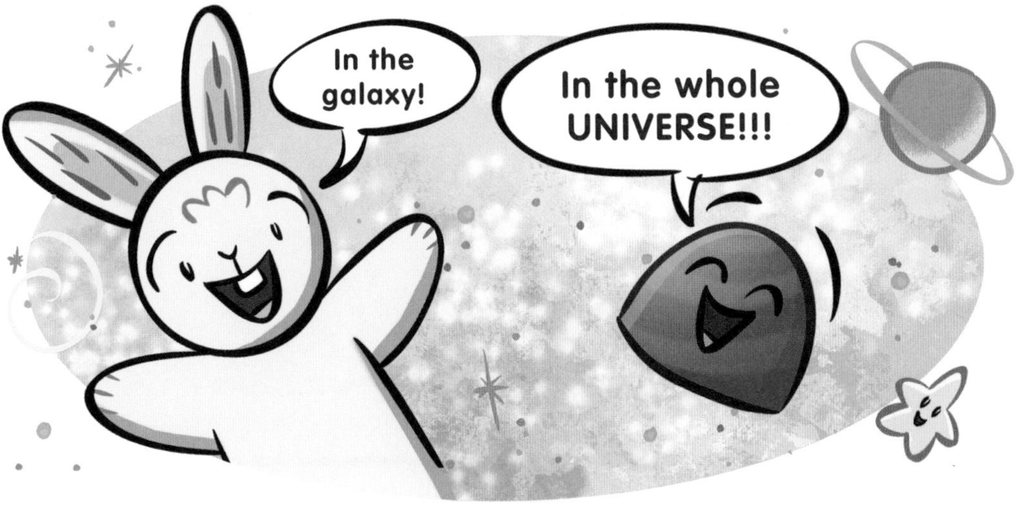
In the galaxy!
In the whole UNIVERSE!!!

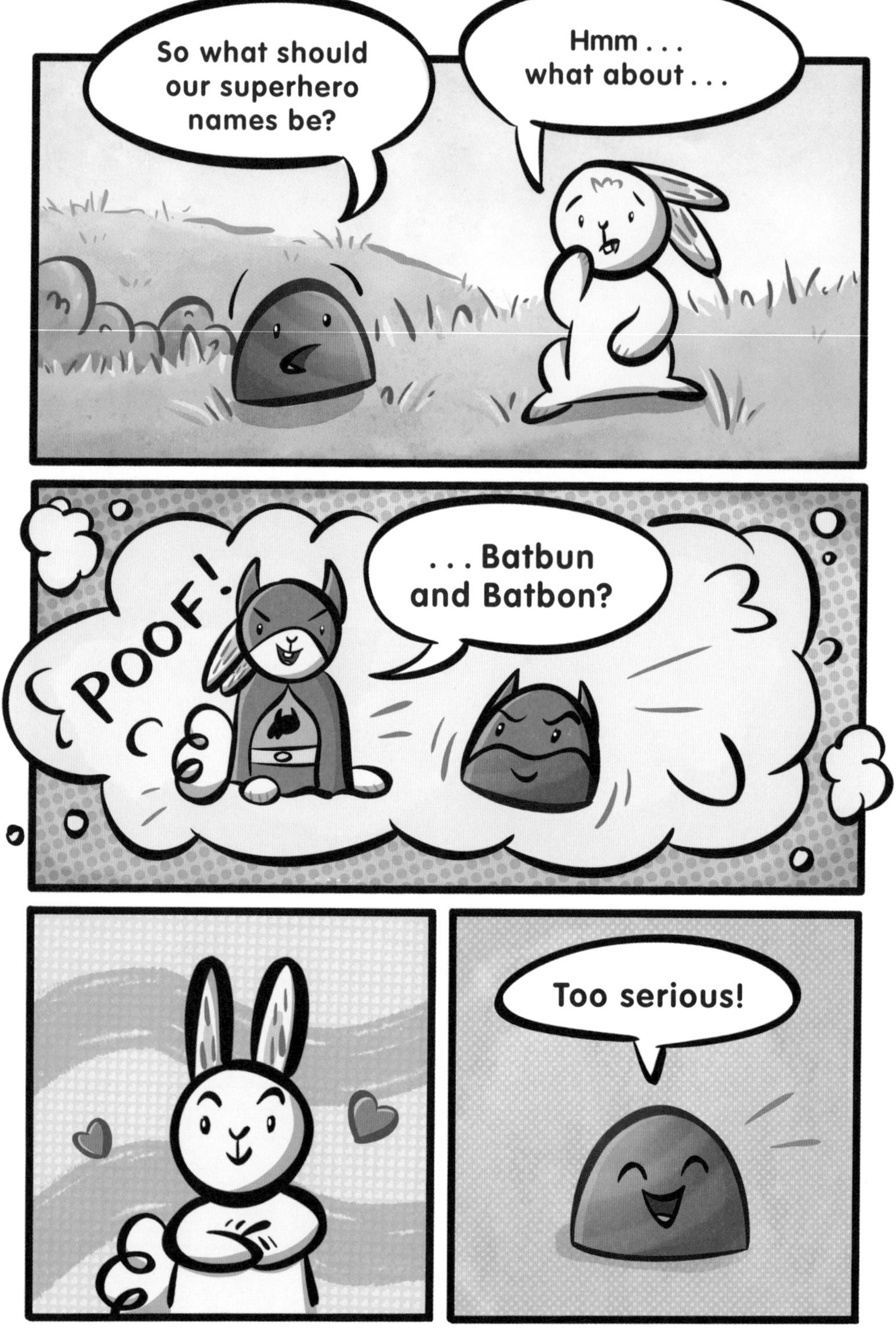
So what should our superhero names be?
Hmm . . . what about . . .
POOF!
. . . Batbun and Batbon?
Too serious!

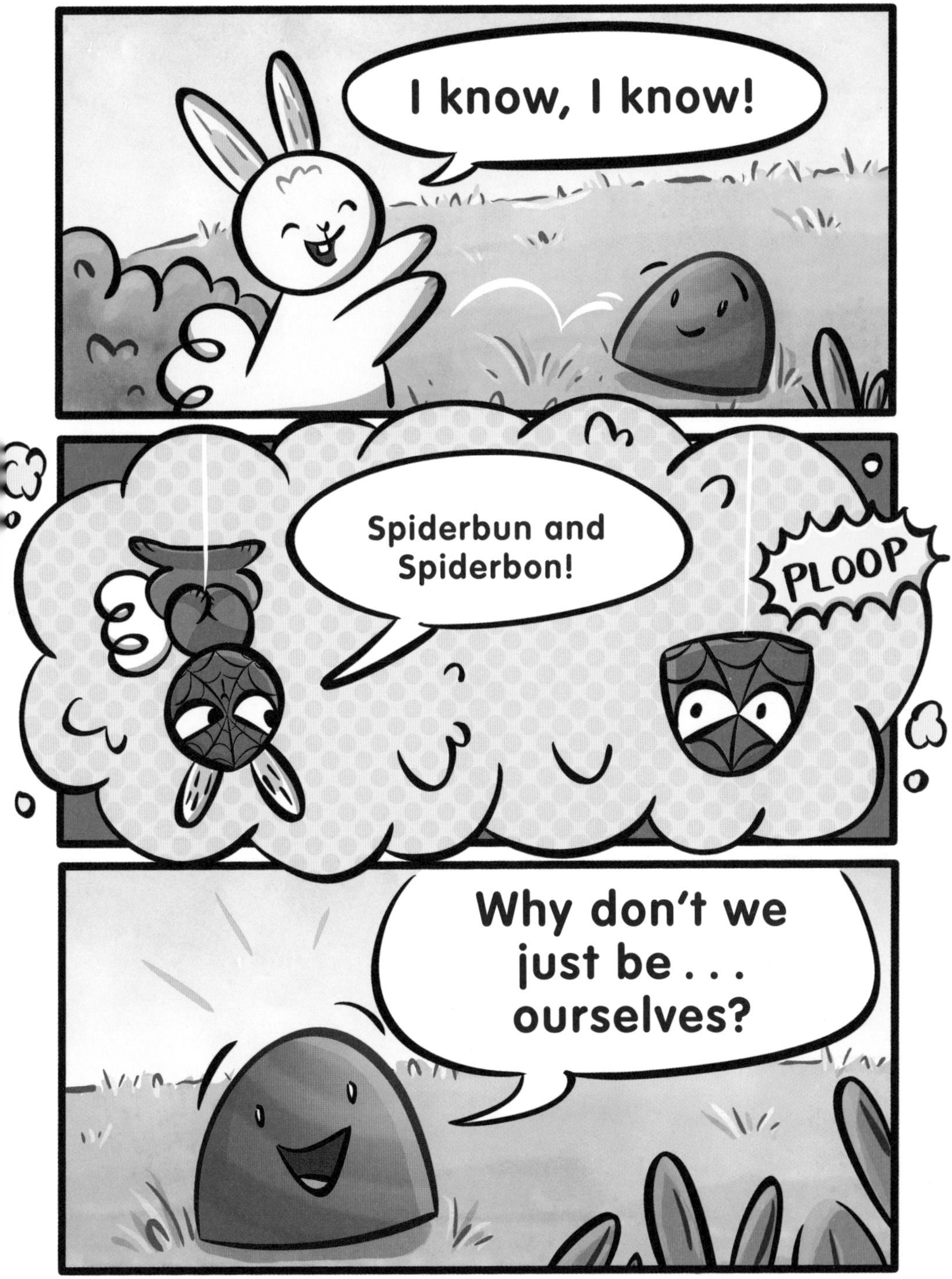
I know, I know!
Spiderbun and Spiderbon!
PLOOP
Why don't we just be . . . ourselves?

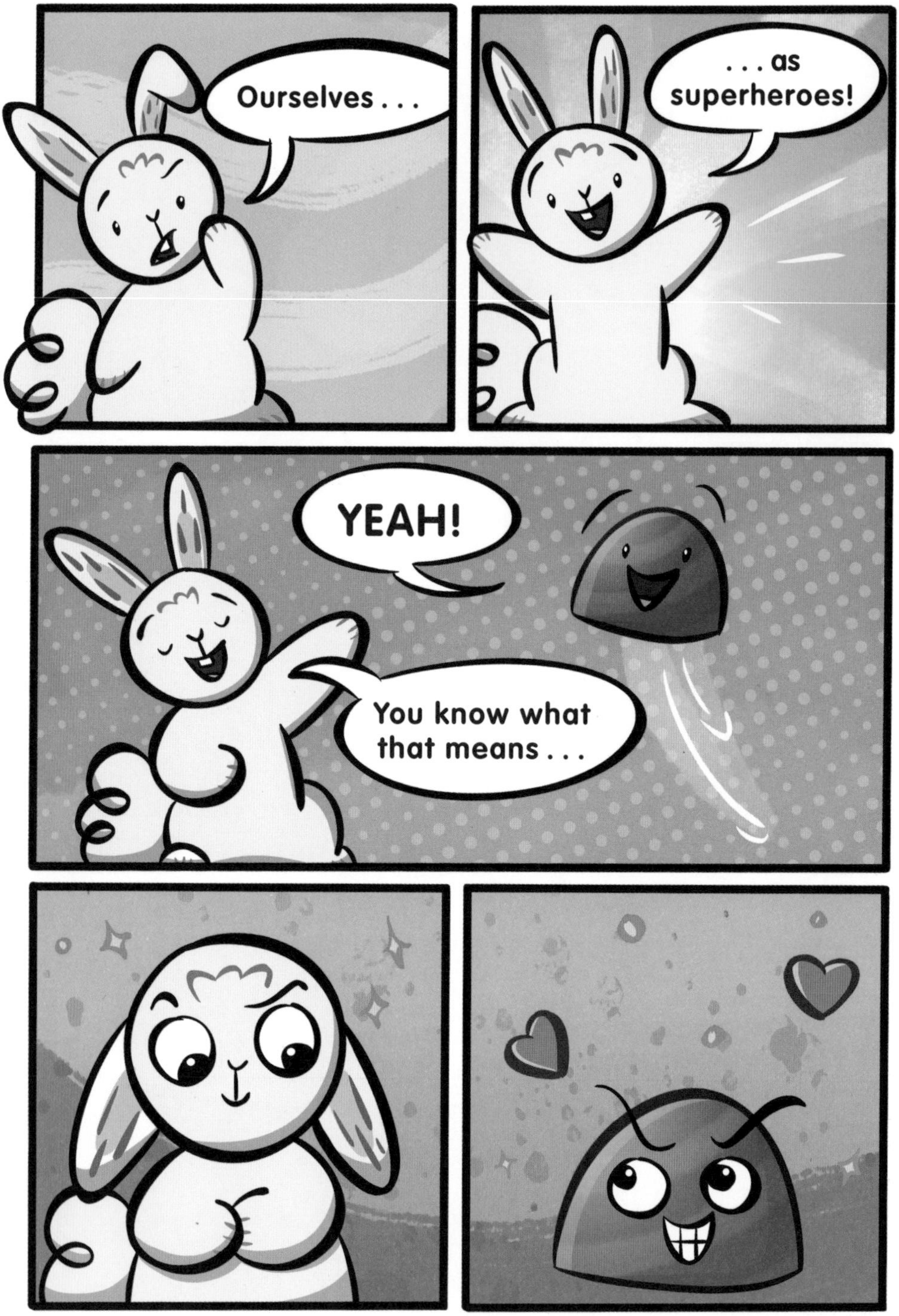

Ourselves . . .
. . . as superheroes!
YEAH!
You know what that means . . .

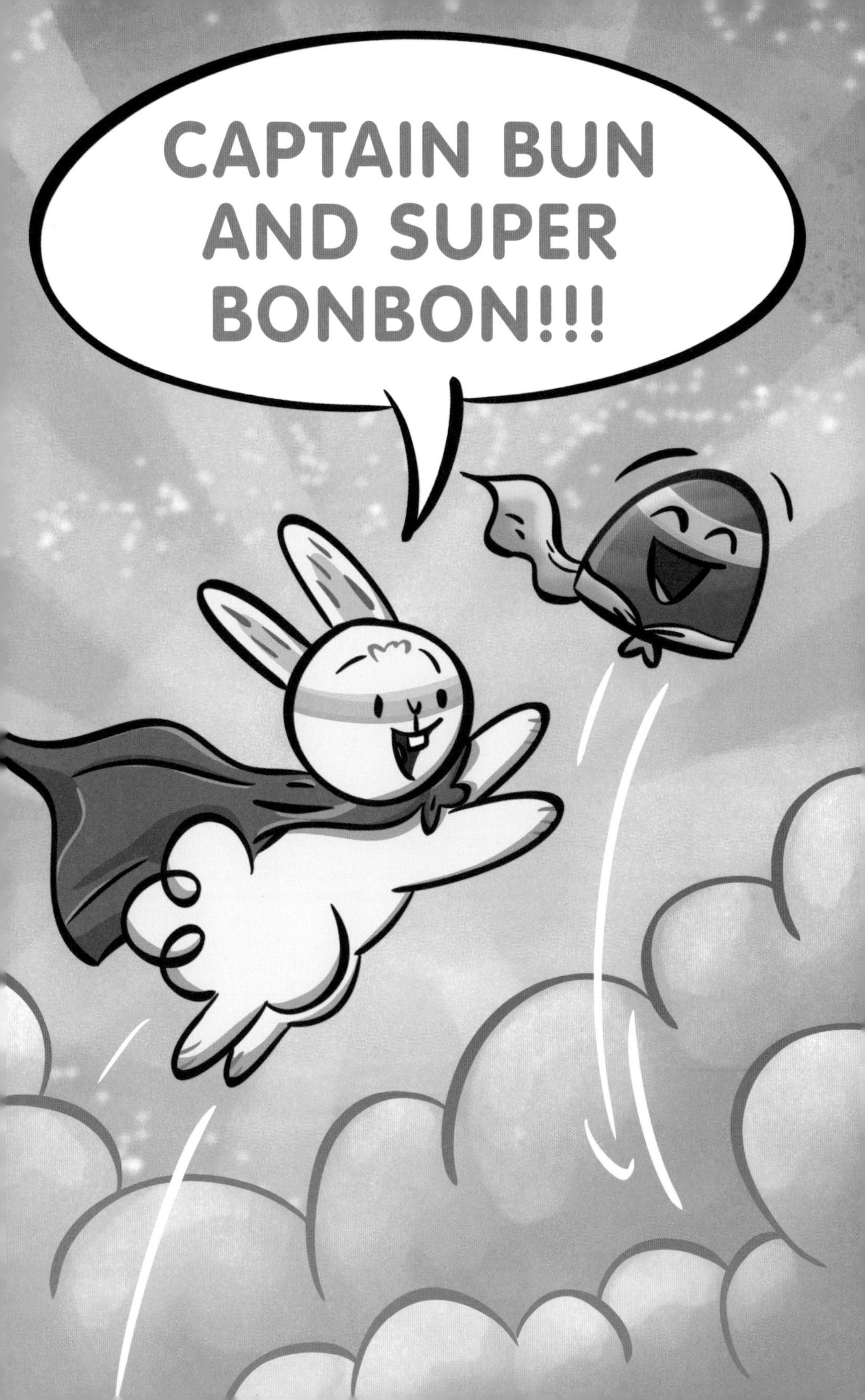
CAPTAIN BUN AND SUPER BONBON!!!

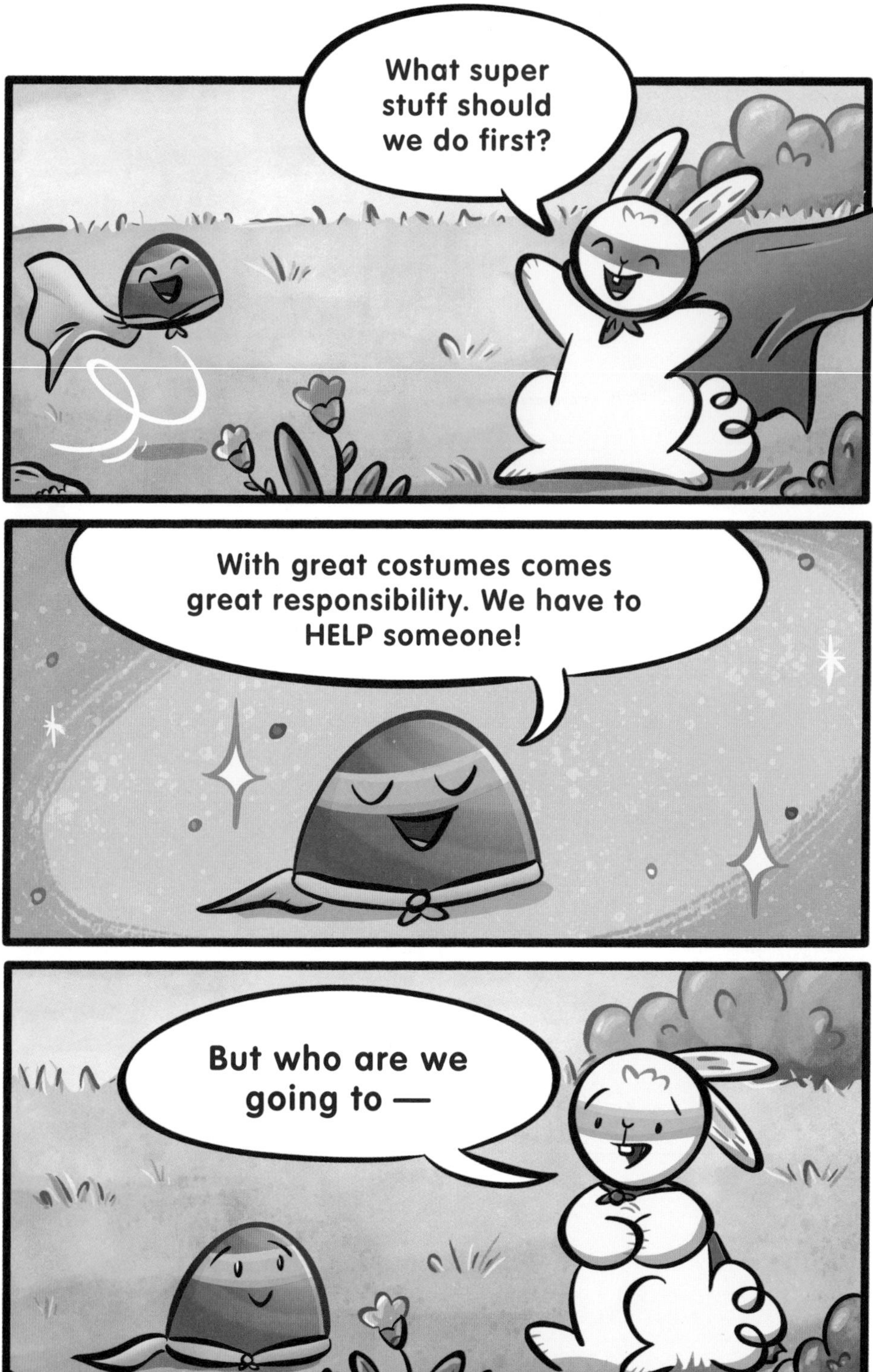
What super stuff should we do first?
With great costumes comes great responsibility. We have to HELP someone!
But who are we going to —

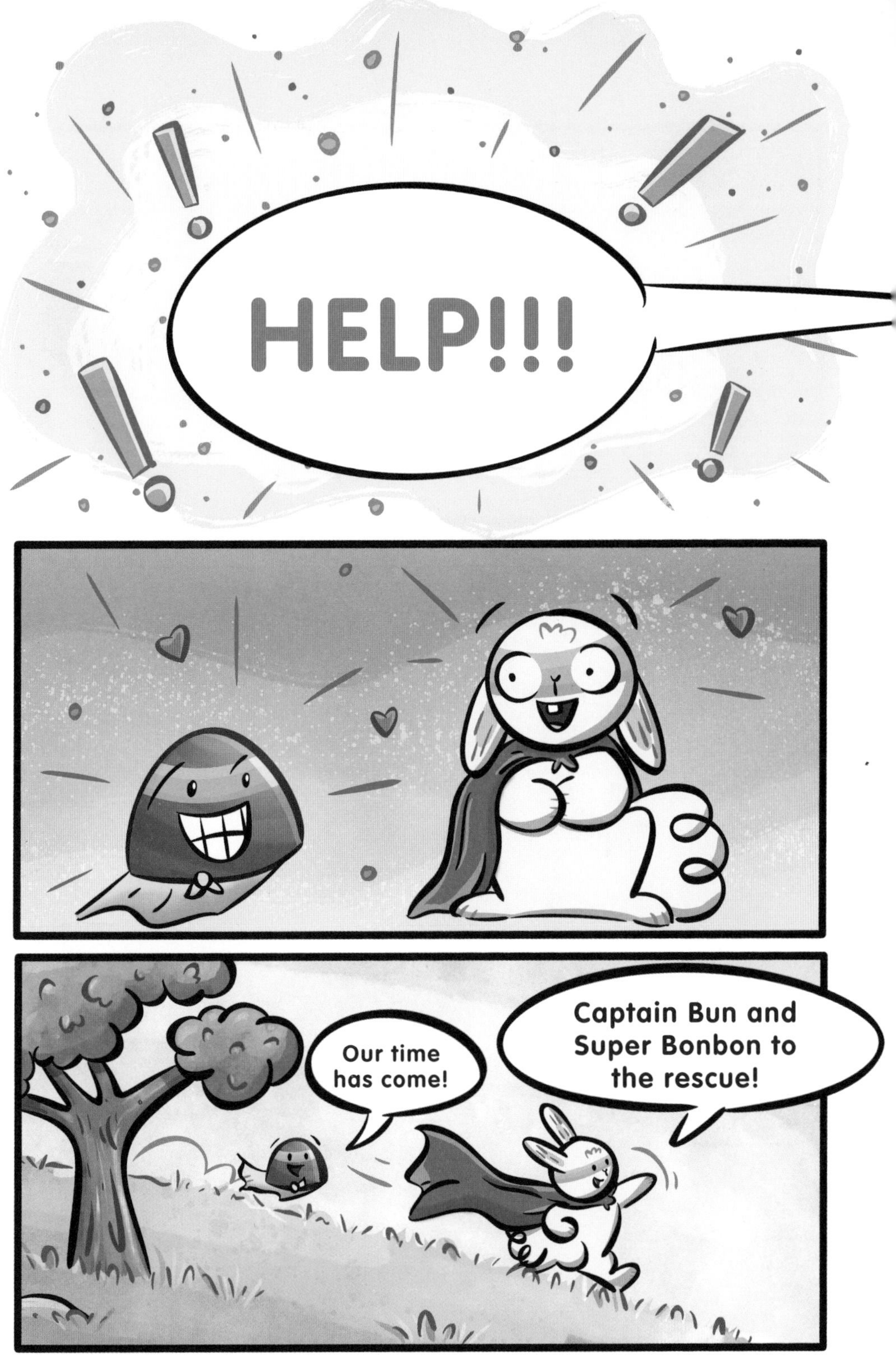
HELP!!!
Our time has come!
Captain Bun and Super Bonbon to the rescue!

BUT THEN . . .

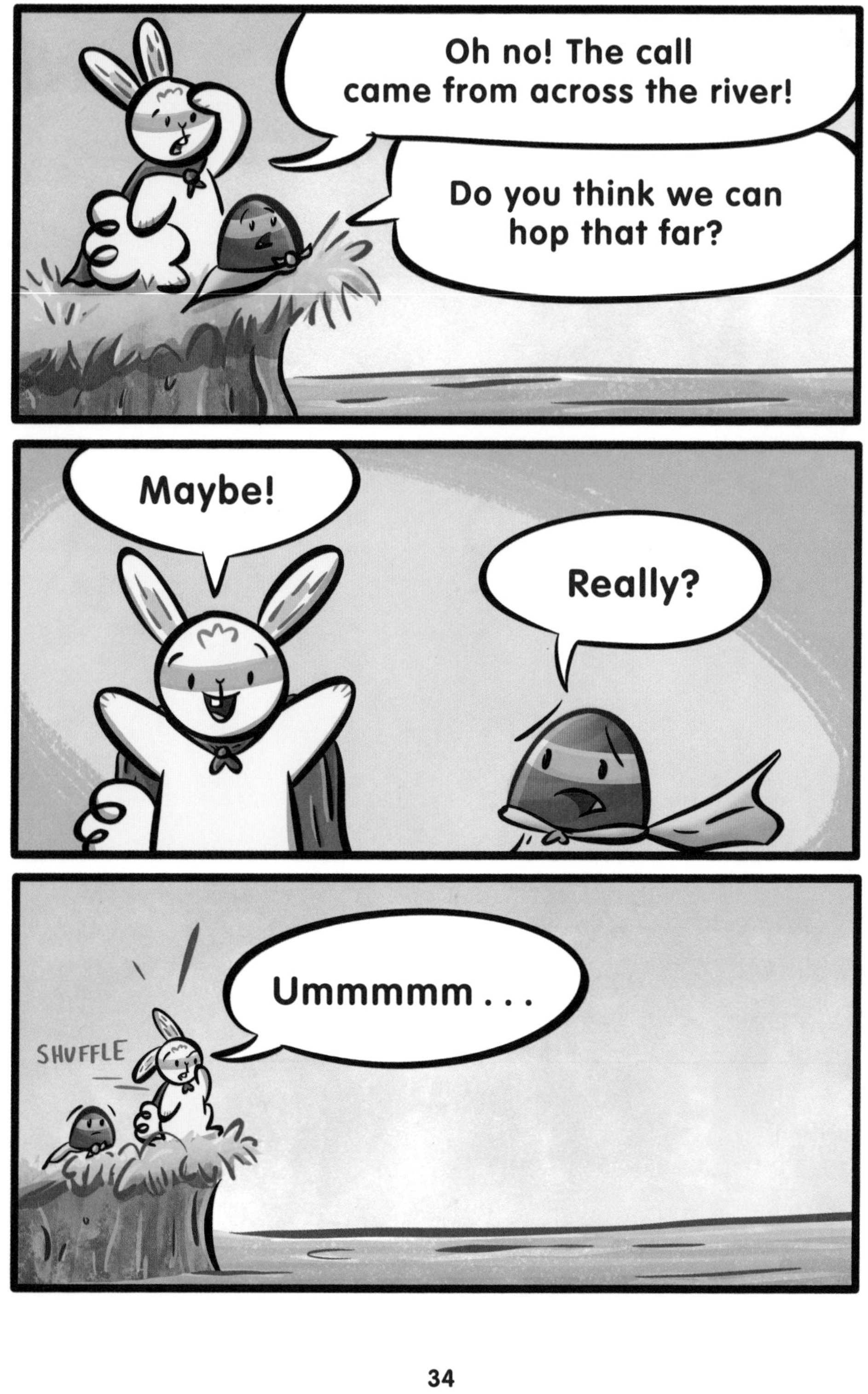
Oh no! The call came from across the river!
Do you think we can hop that far?
Maybe!
Really?
SHUFFLE
Ummmmm . . .

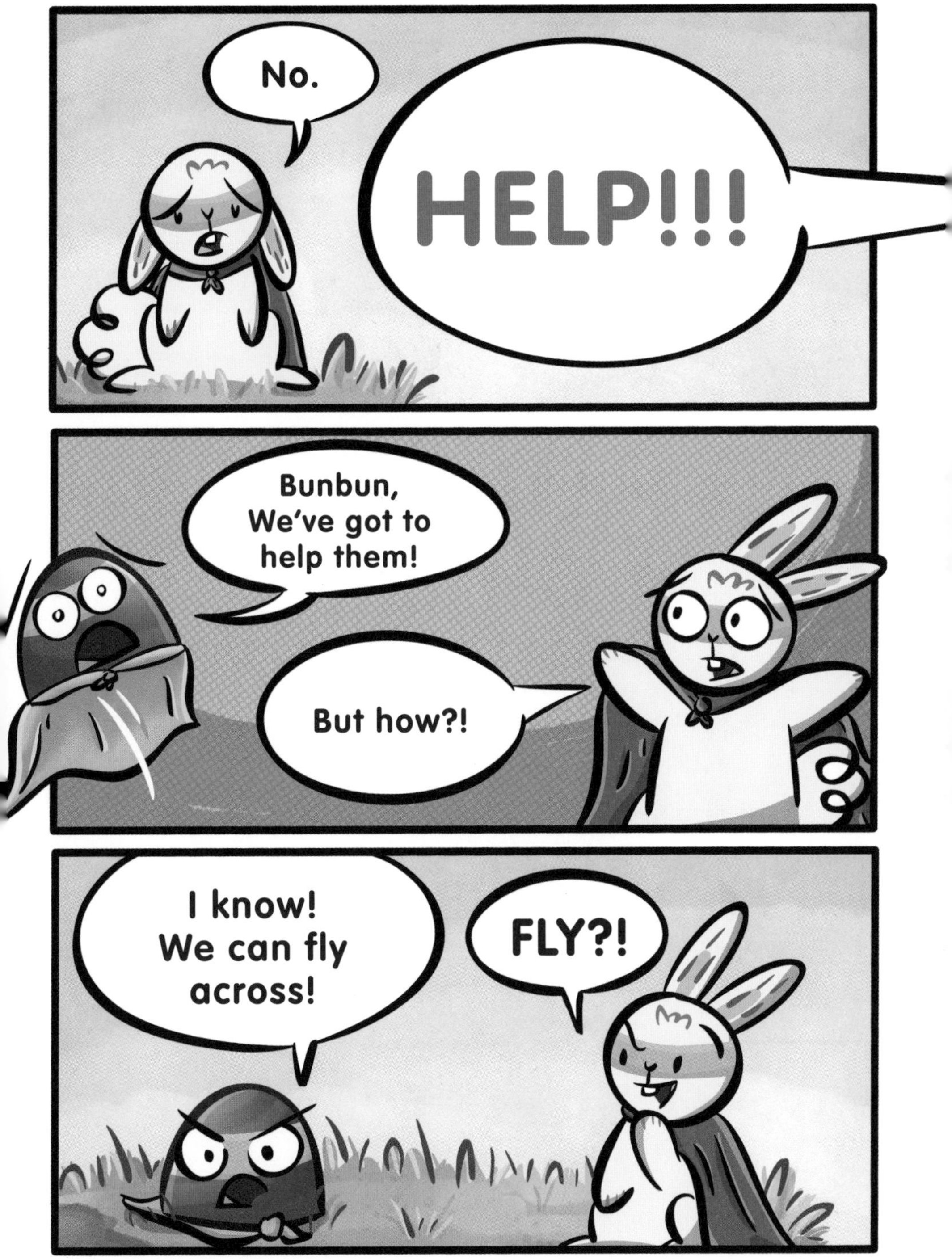
No.
HELP!!!
Bunbun, We've got to help them!
But how?!
I know! We can fly across!
FLY?!

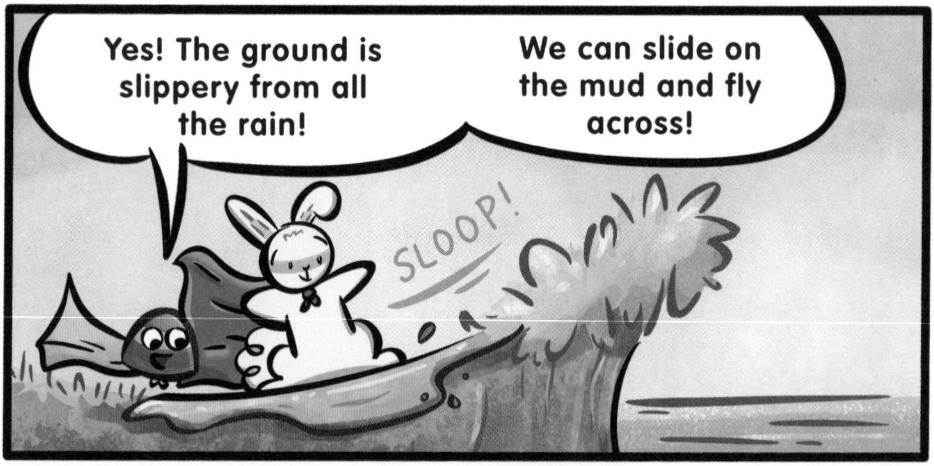
Yes! The ground is slippery from all the rain!
We can slide on the mud and fly across!
SLOOP!

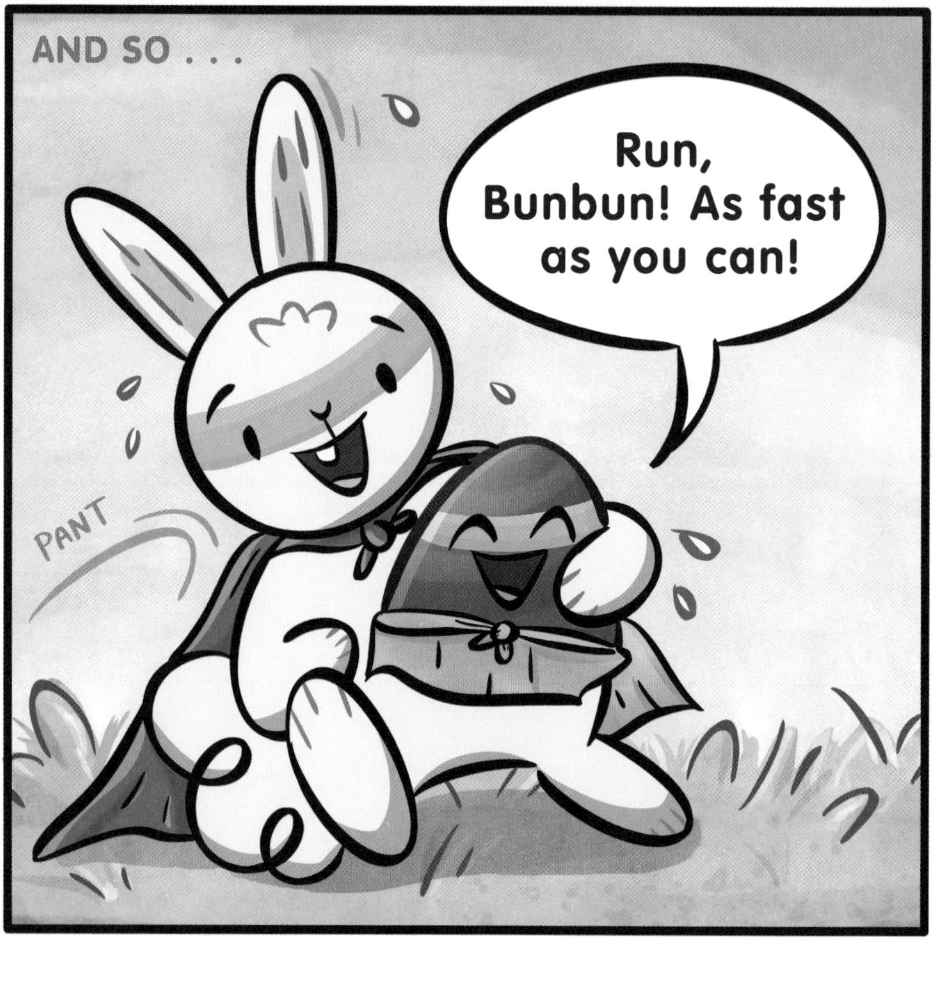
AND SO . . .
Run, Bunbun! As fast as you can!
PANT

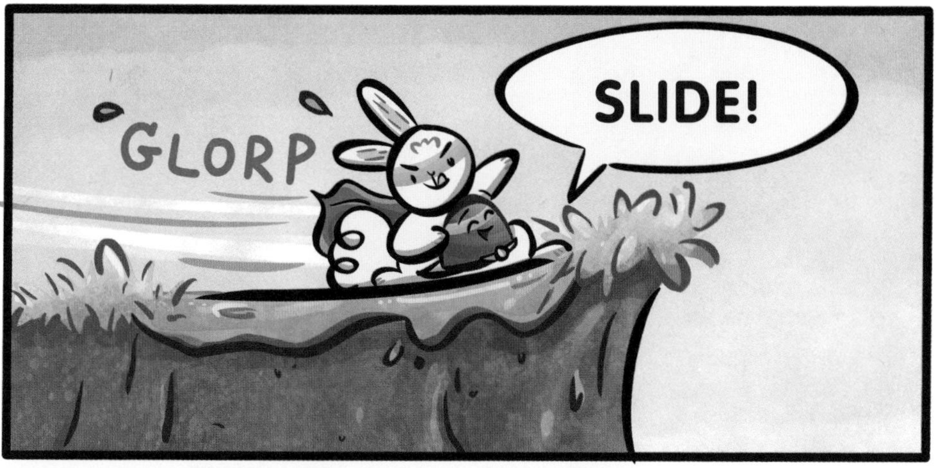
GLORP
SLIDE!

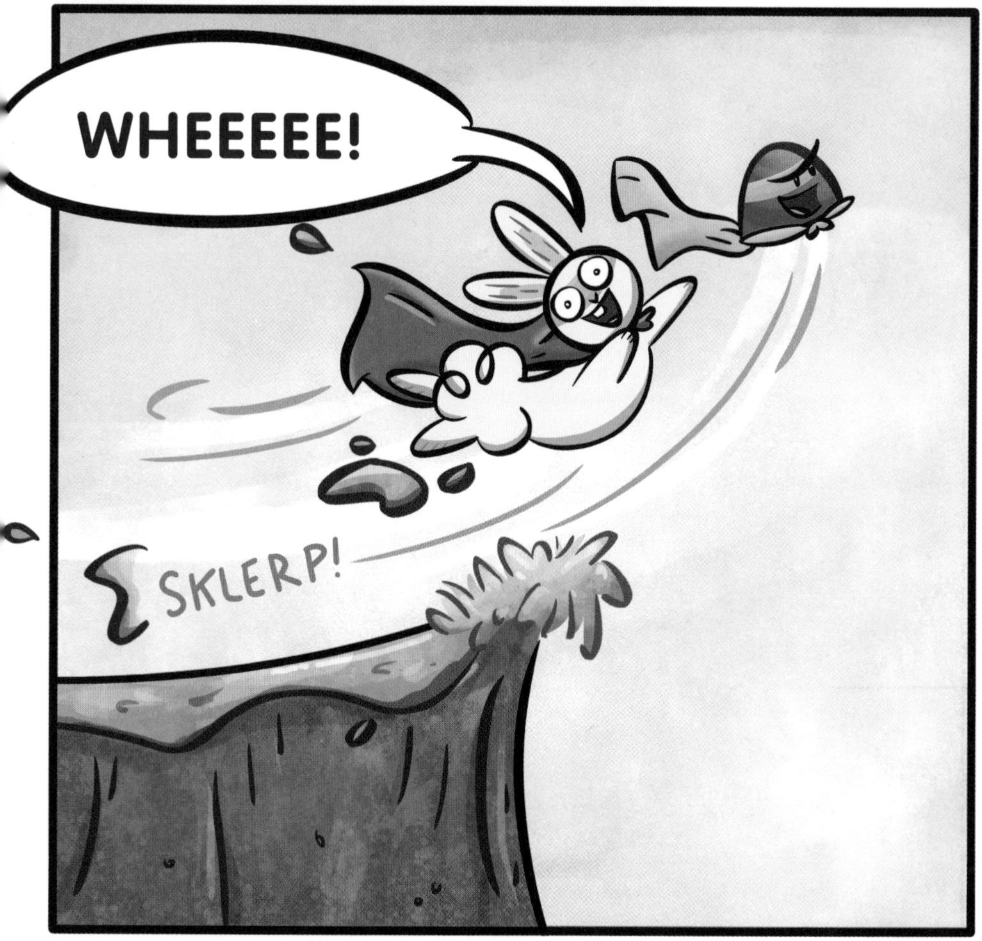
WHEEEEE!
SKLERP!

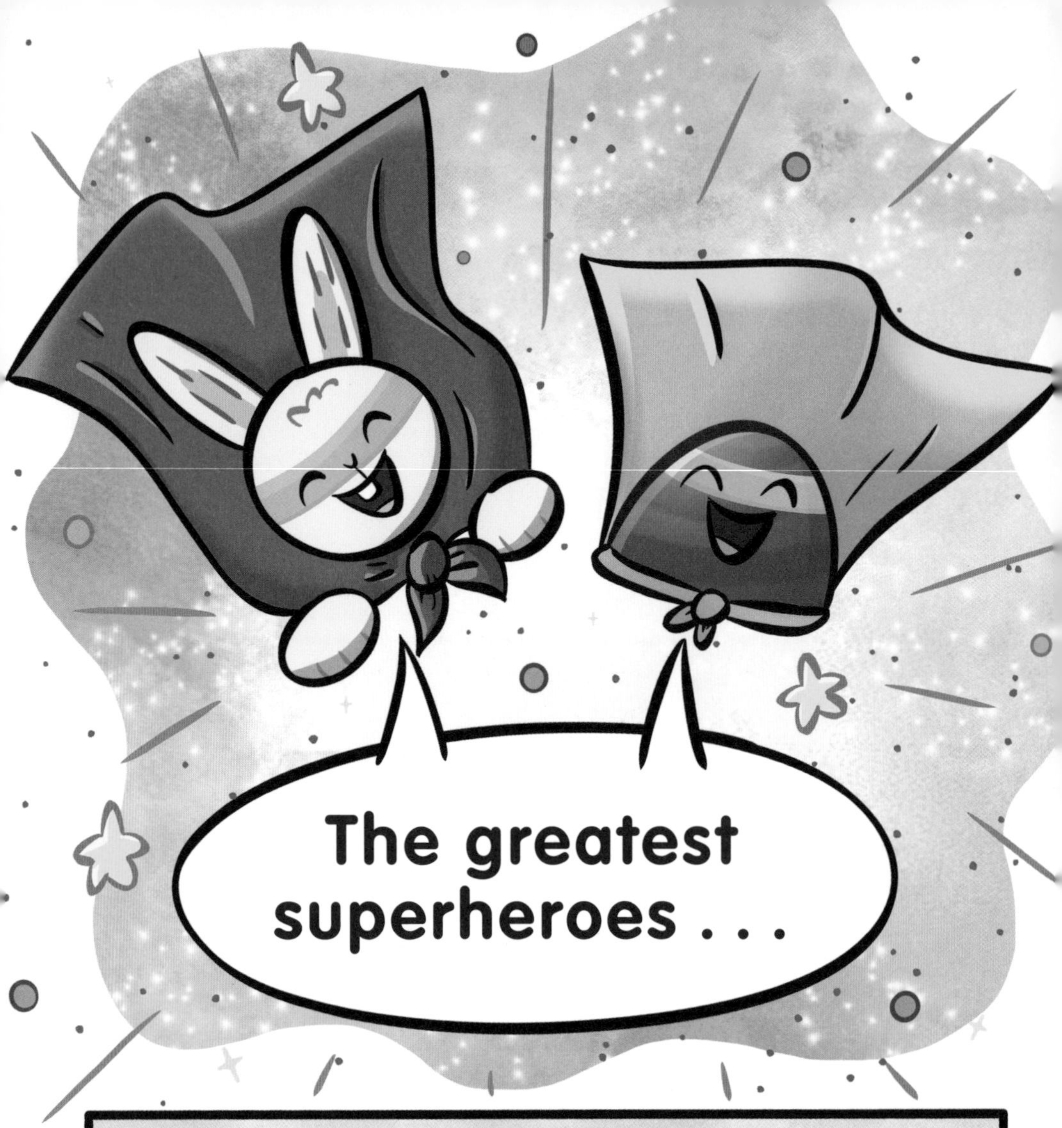
The greatest superheroes . . .

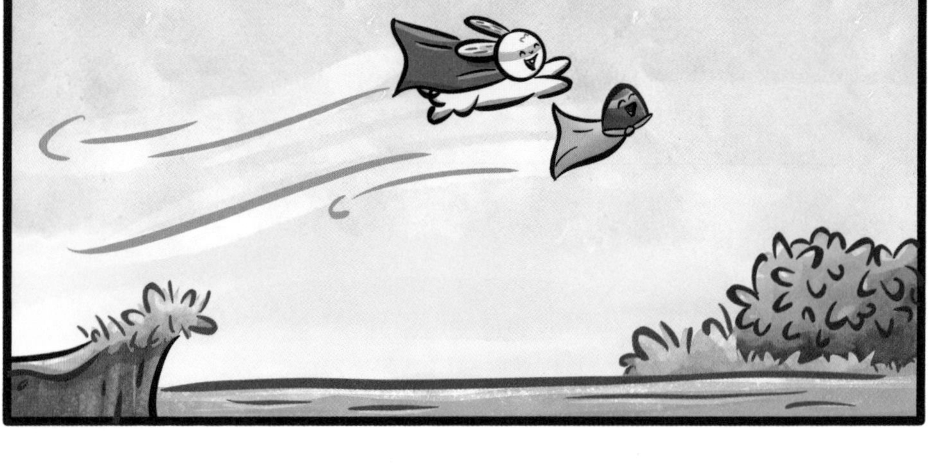

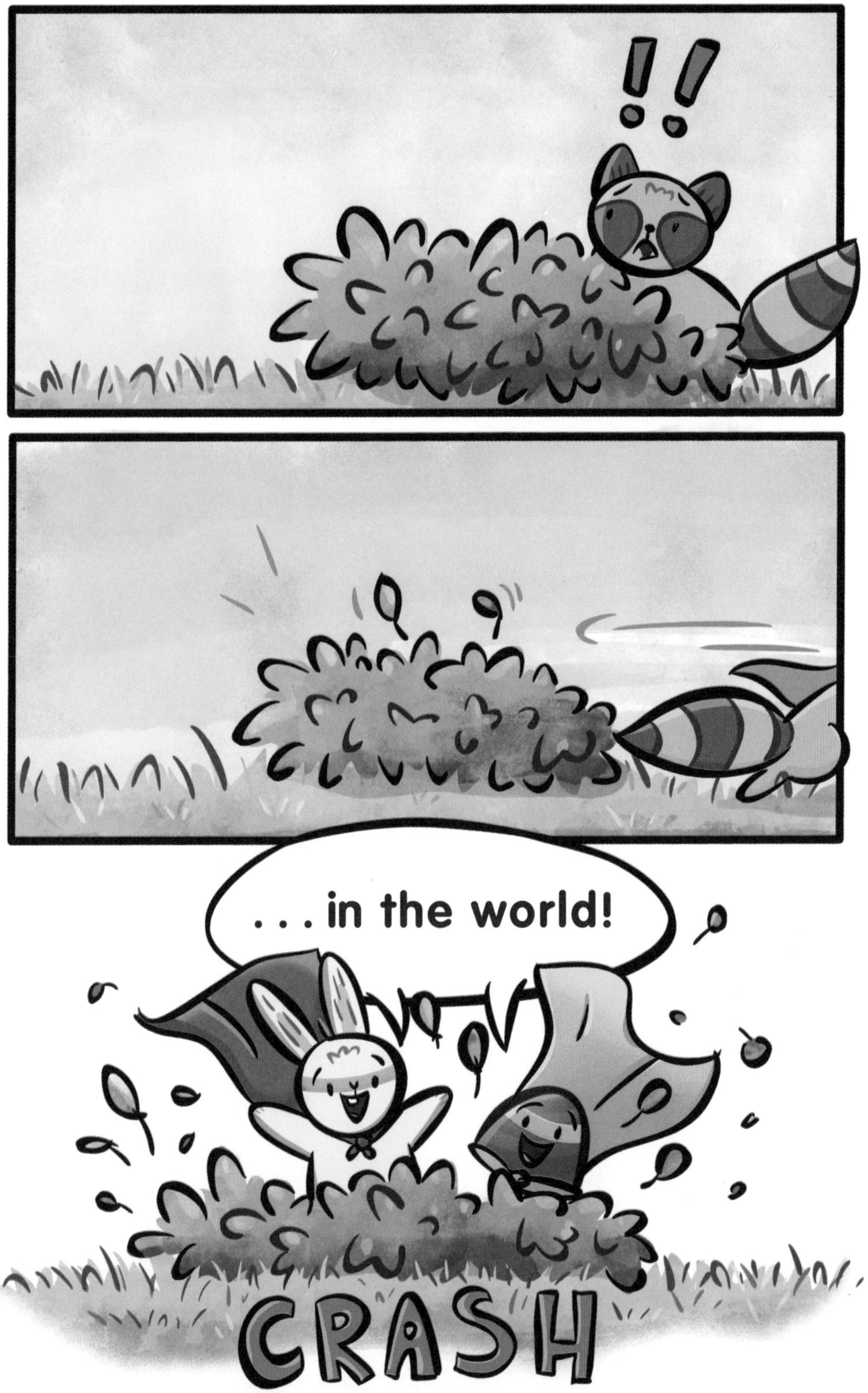
!!
. . . in the world!
CRASH

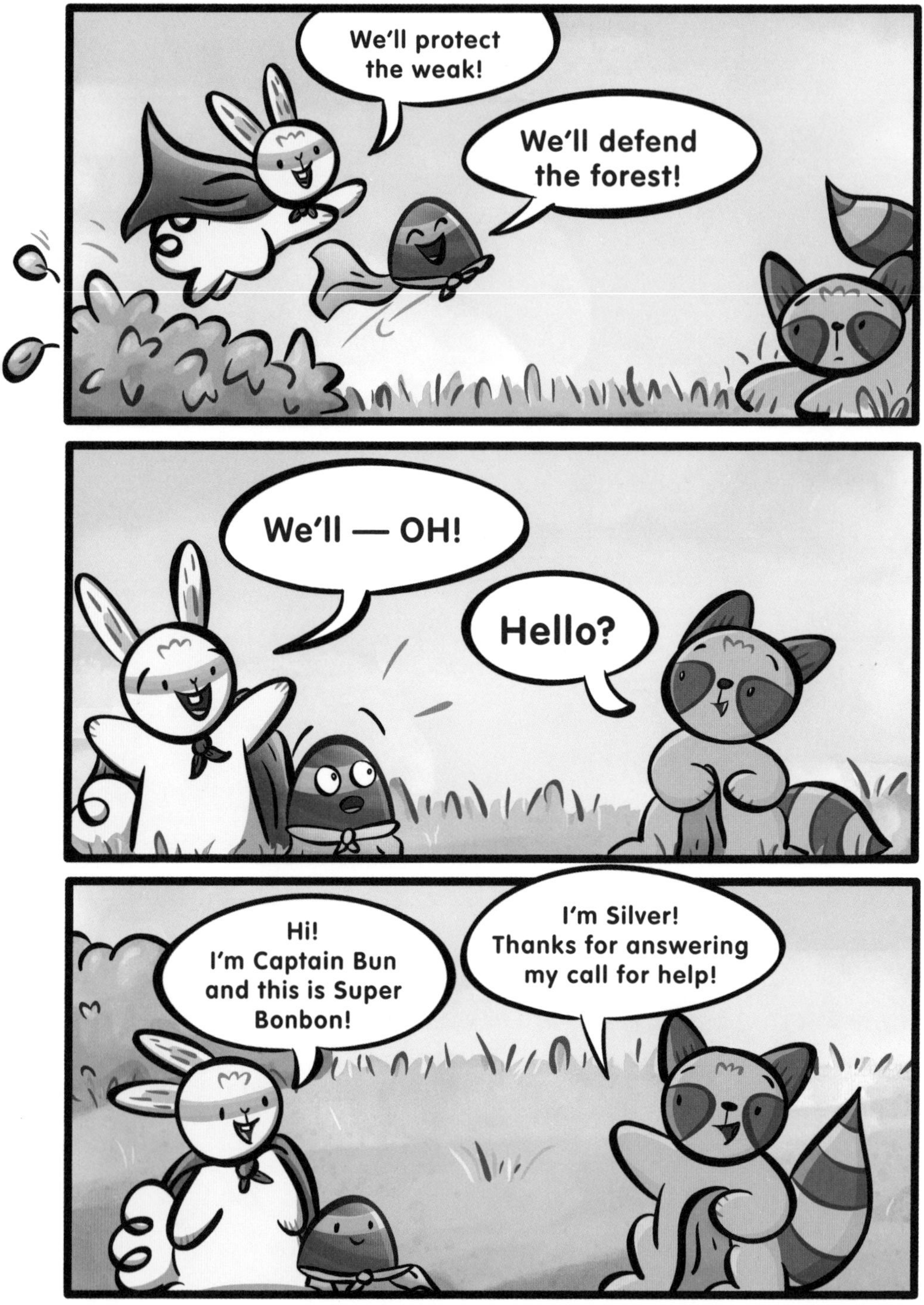
We'll protect the weak!
We'll defend the forest!
We'll — OH!
Hello?
Hi! I'm Captain Bun and this is Super Bonbon!
I'm Silver! Thanks for answering my call for help!

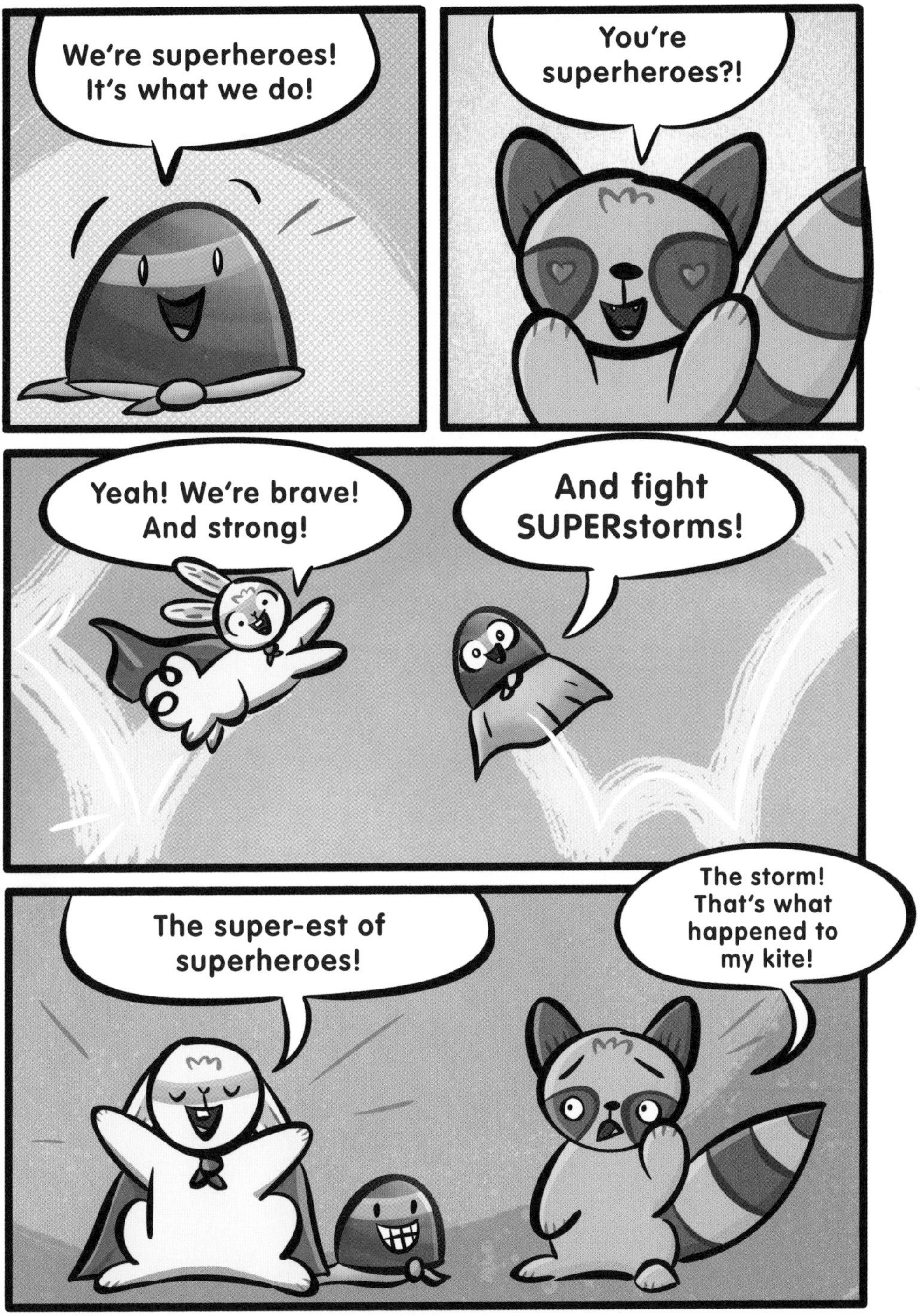
We're superheroes! It's what we do!
You're superheroes?!
Yeah! We're brave! And strong!
And fight SUPERstorms!
The super-est of superheroes!
The storm! That's what happened to my kite!

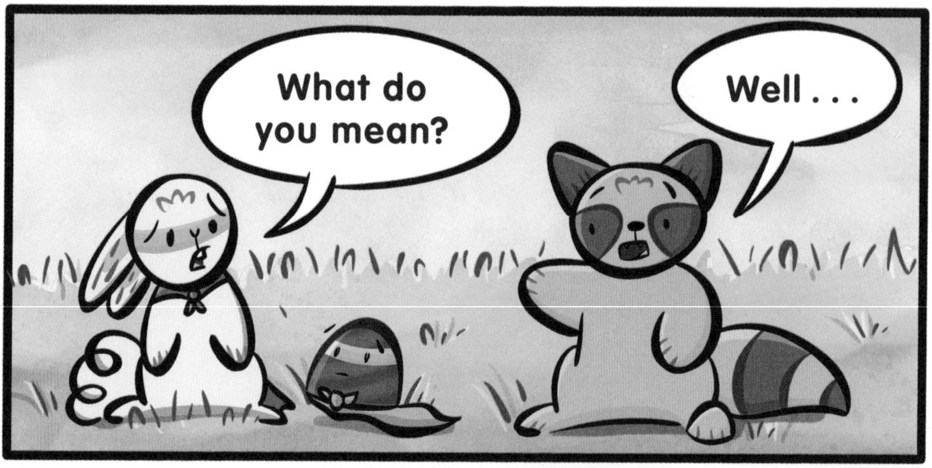
What do you mean?
Well . . .

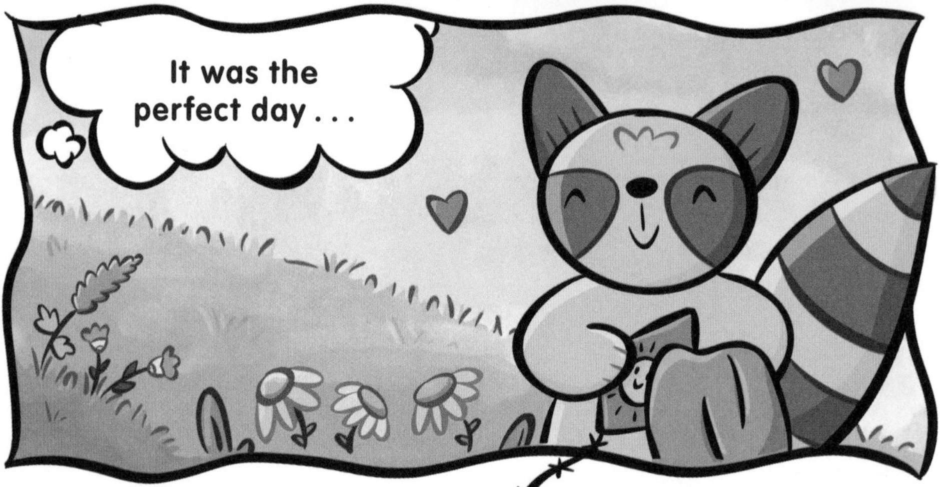
It was the perfect day . . .

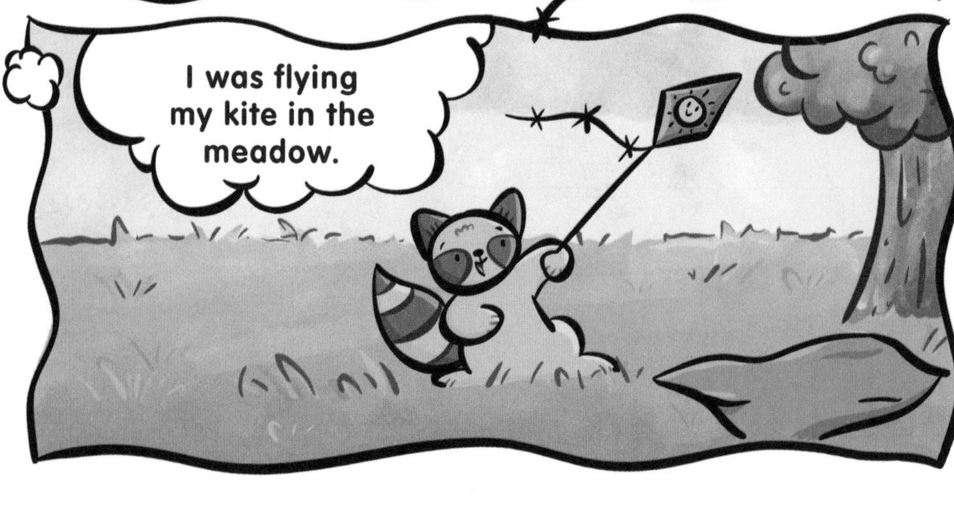
I was flying my kite in the meadow.

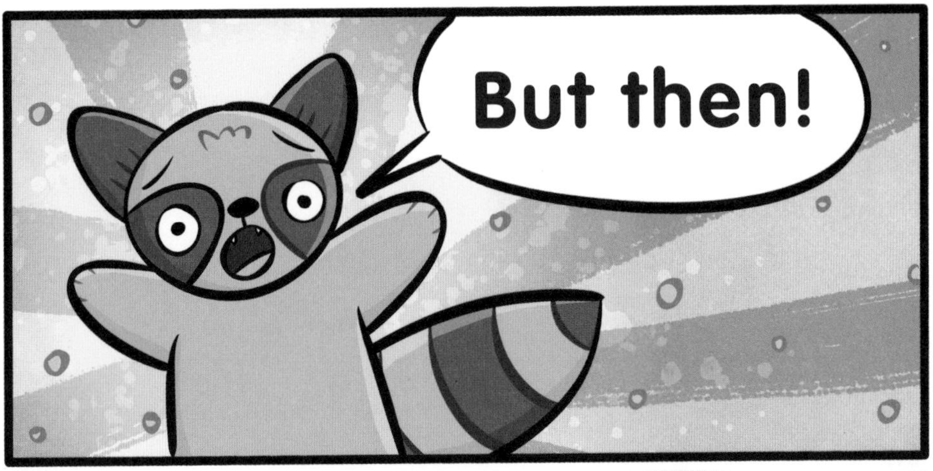
But then!

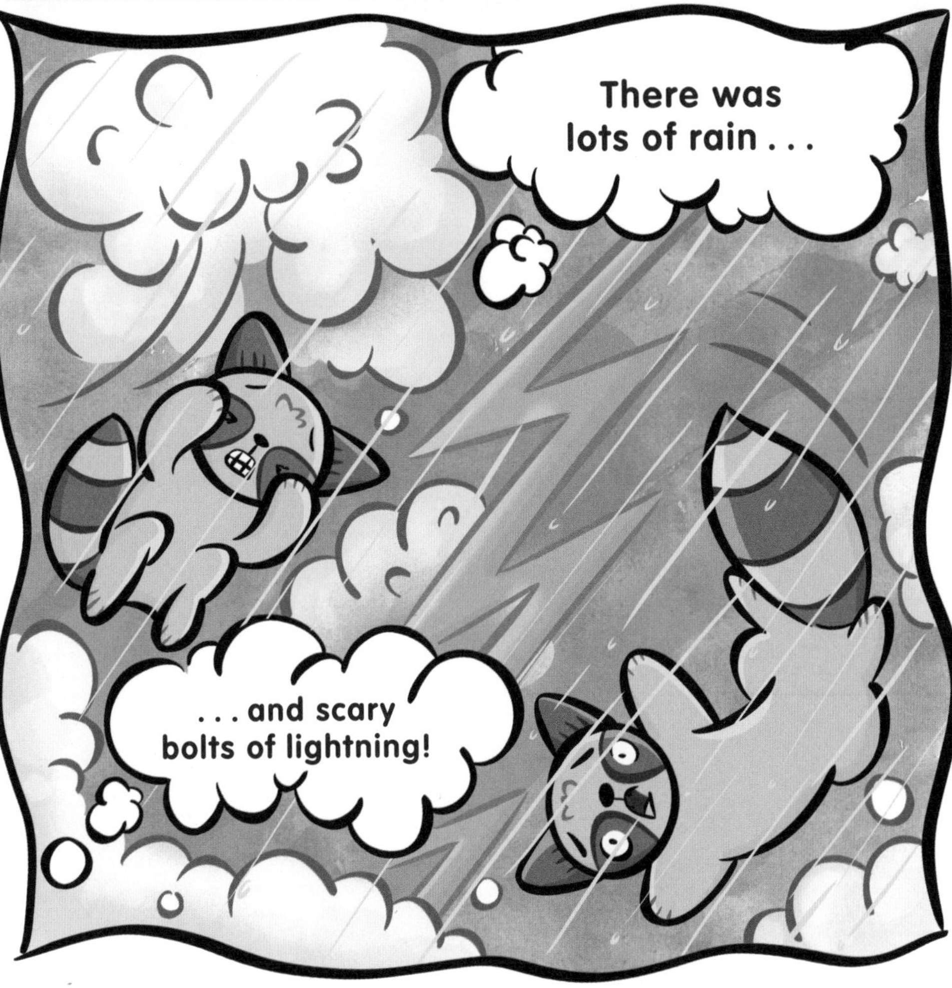
There was lots of rain . . .
. . . and scary bolts of lightning!

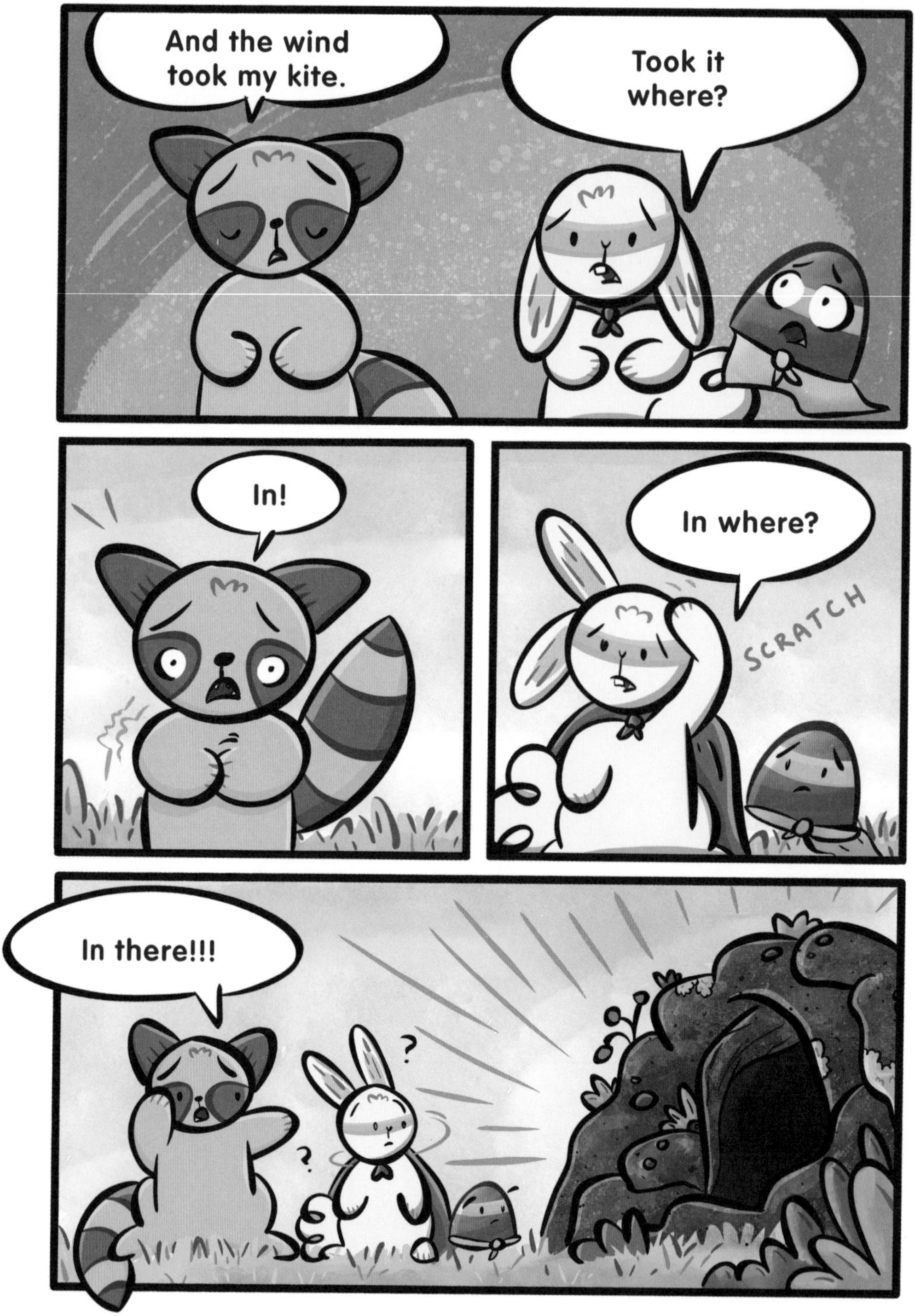
And the wind took my kite.
Took it where?
In!
In where?
SCRATCH
In there!!!

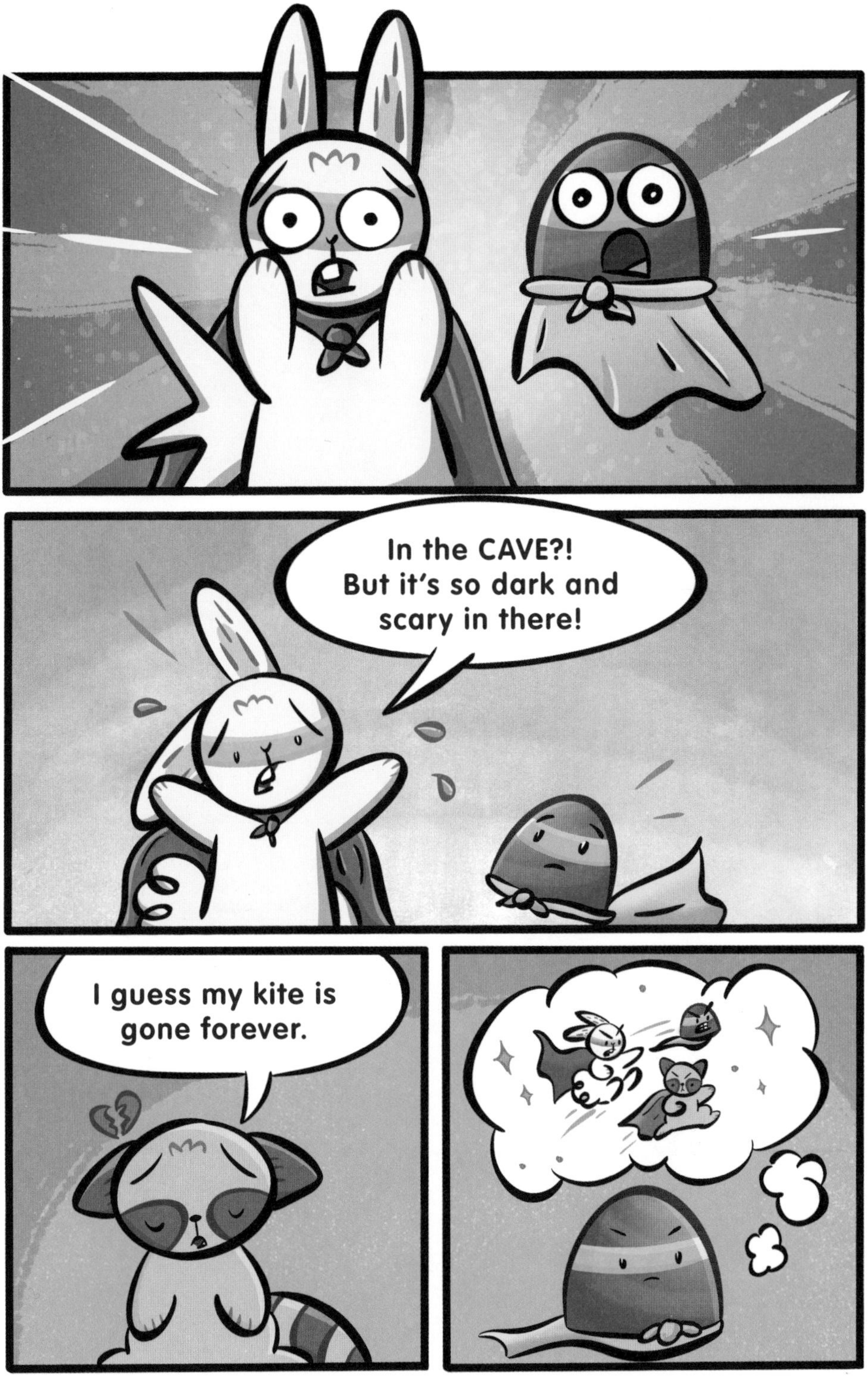
In the CAVE?! But it's so dark and scary in there!
I guess my kite is gone forever.

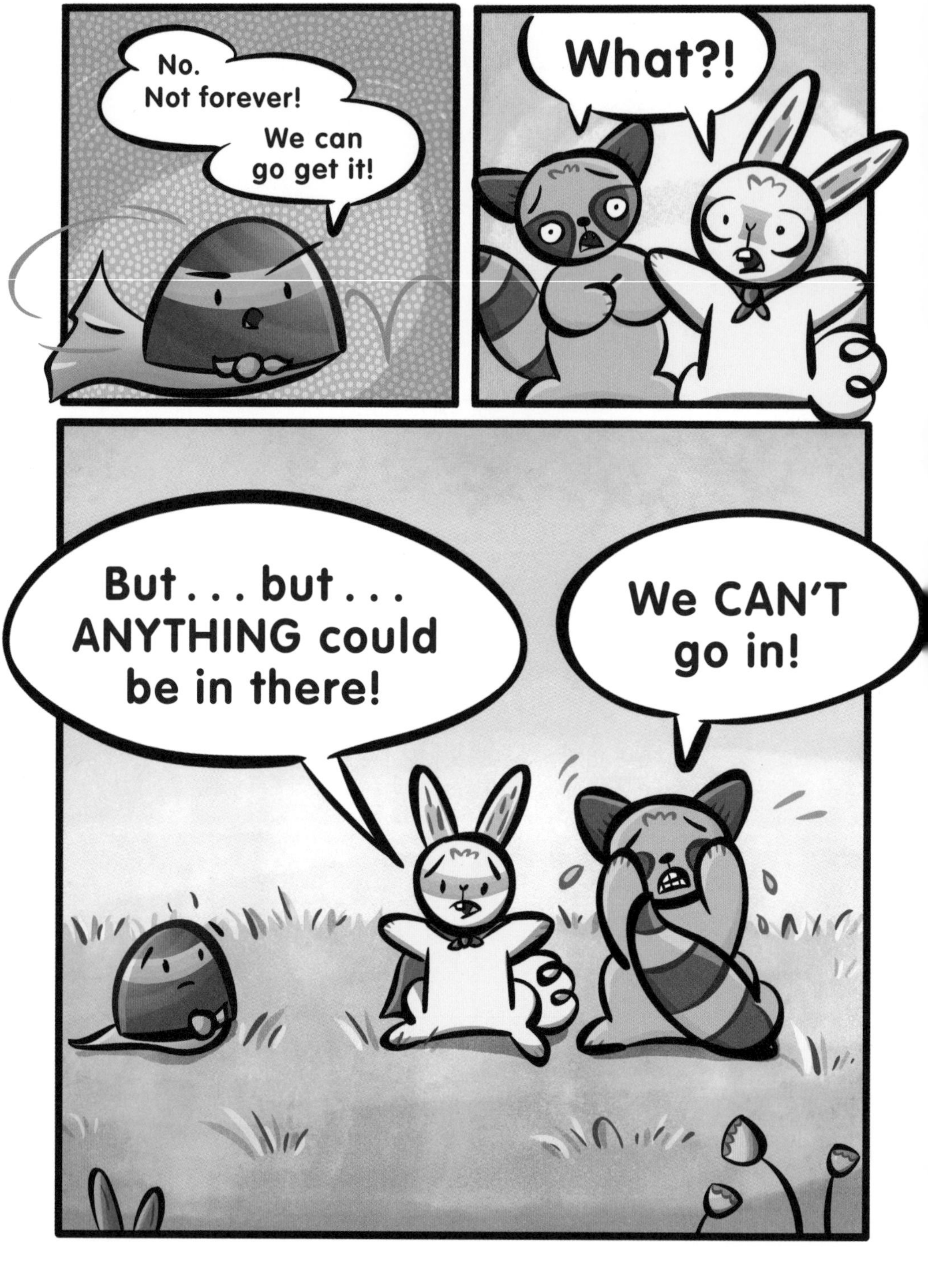
No.
Not forever!
We can
go get it!
What?!
But . . . but . . .
ANYTHING could
be in there!
We CAN'T
go in!

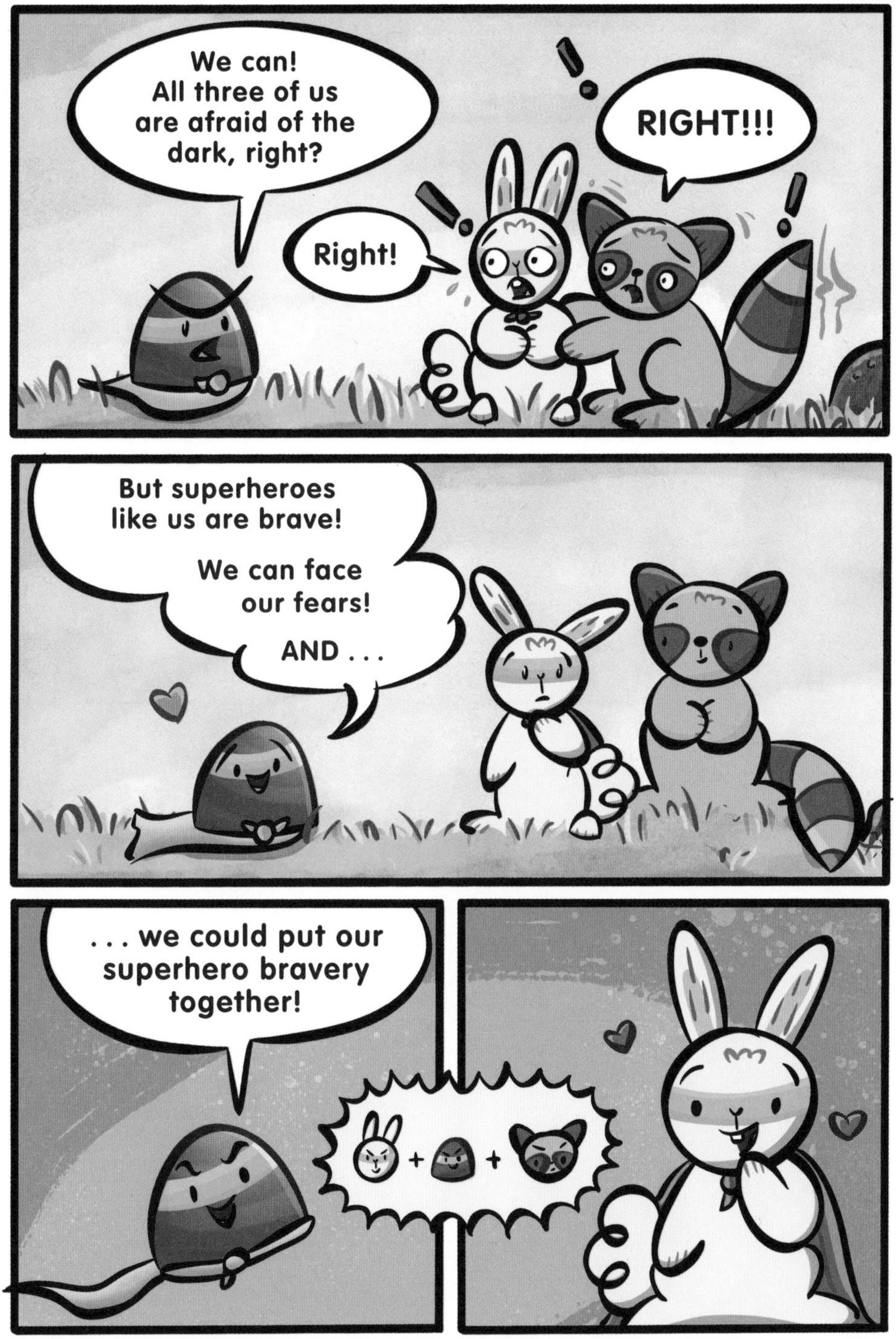
We can!
All three of us are afraid of the dark, right?
Right!
RIGHT!!!
But superheroes like us are brave!
We can face our fears!
AND . . .
. . . we could put our superhero bravery together!
+
+

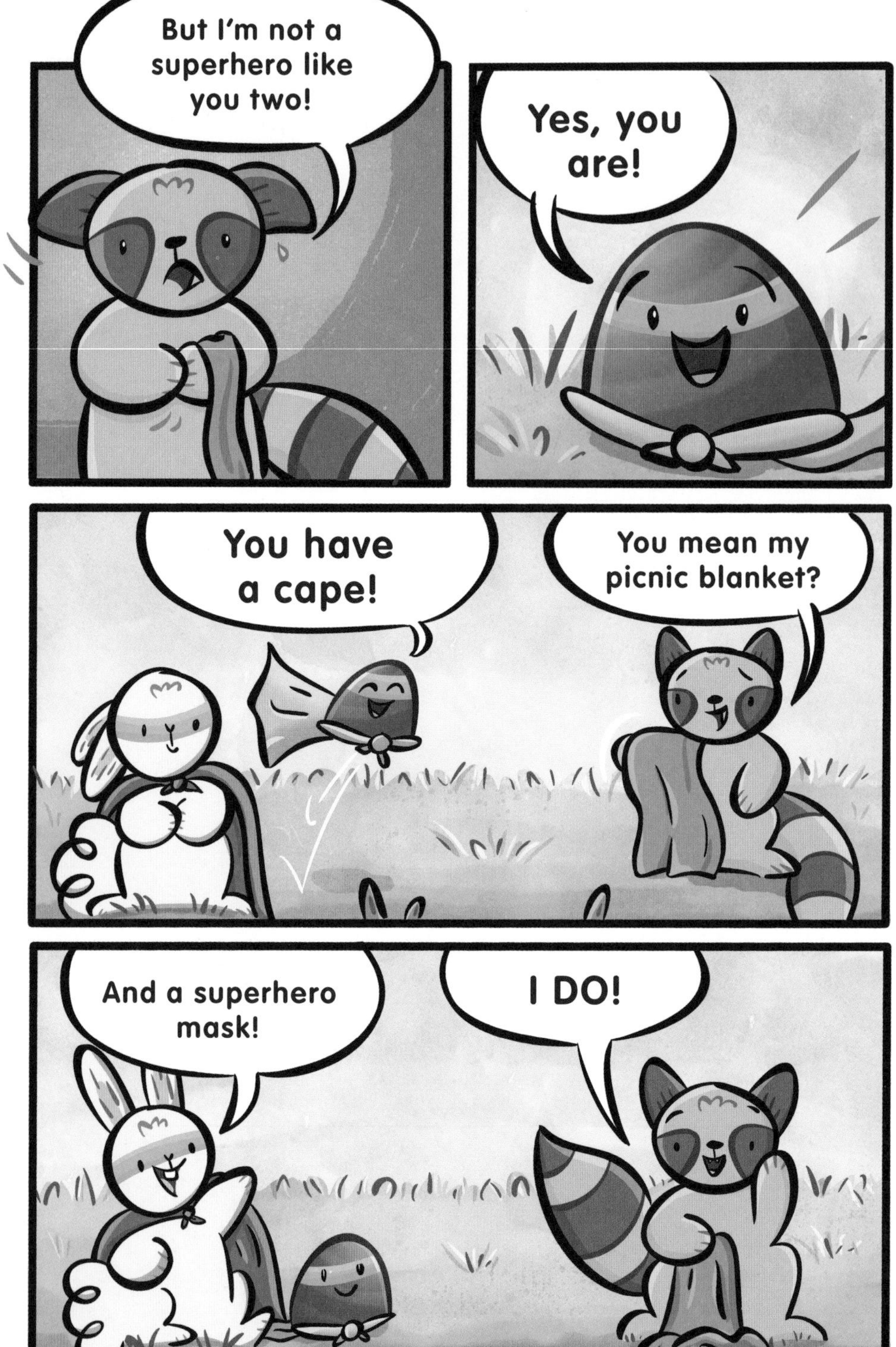
But I'm not a superhero like you two!
Yes, you are!
You have a cape!
You mean my picnic blanket?
And a superhero mask!
I DO!

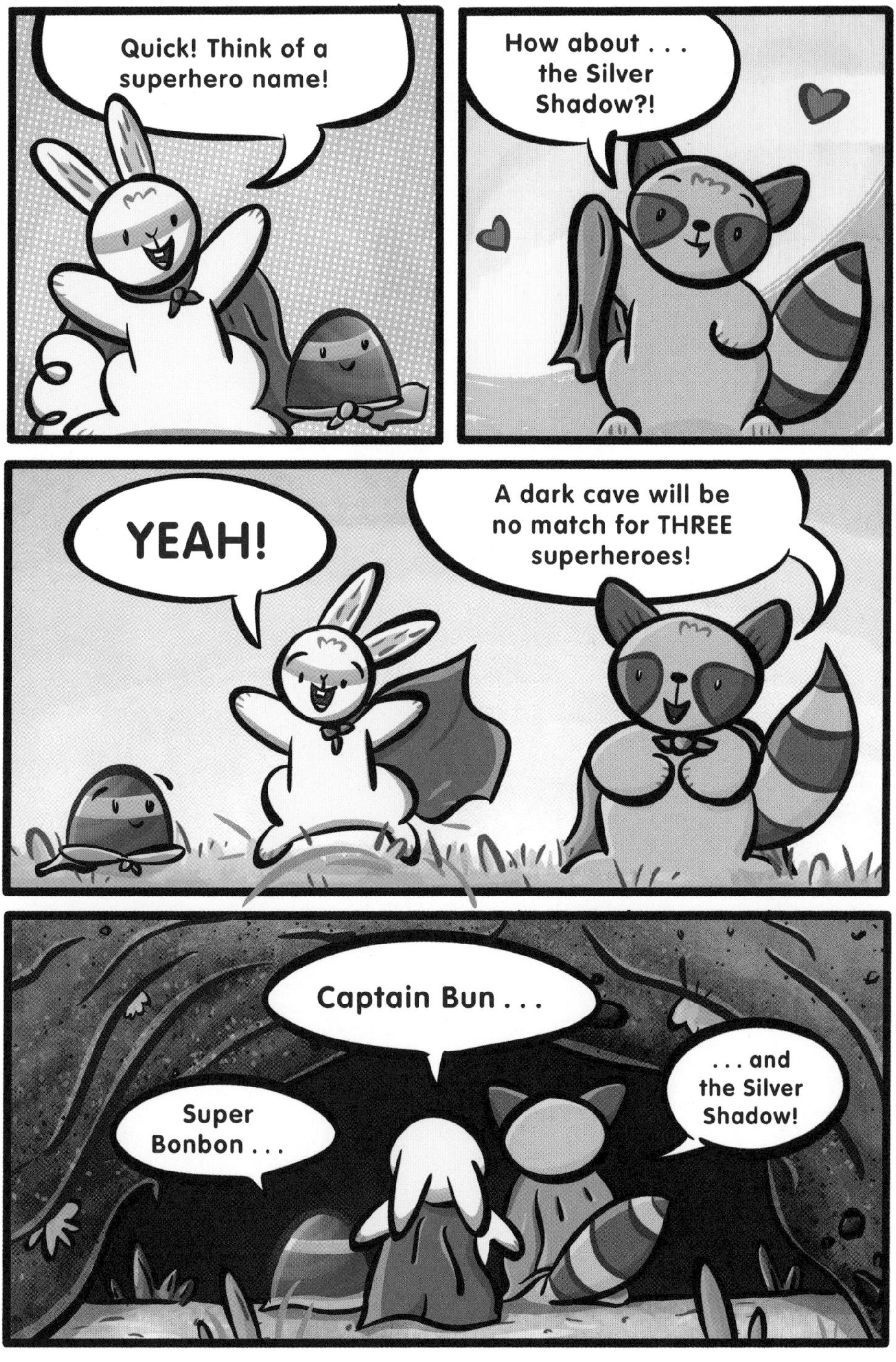
Quick! Think of a superhero name!
How about . . . the Silver Shadow?!
YEAH!
A dark cave will be no match for THREE superheroes!
Captain Bun . . .
Super Bonbon . . .
. . . and the Silver Shadow!

AND SO . . .

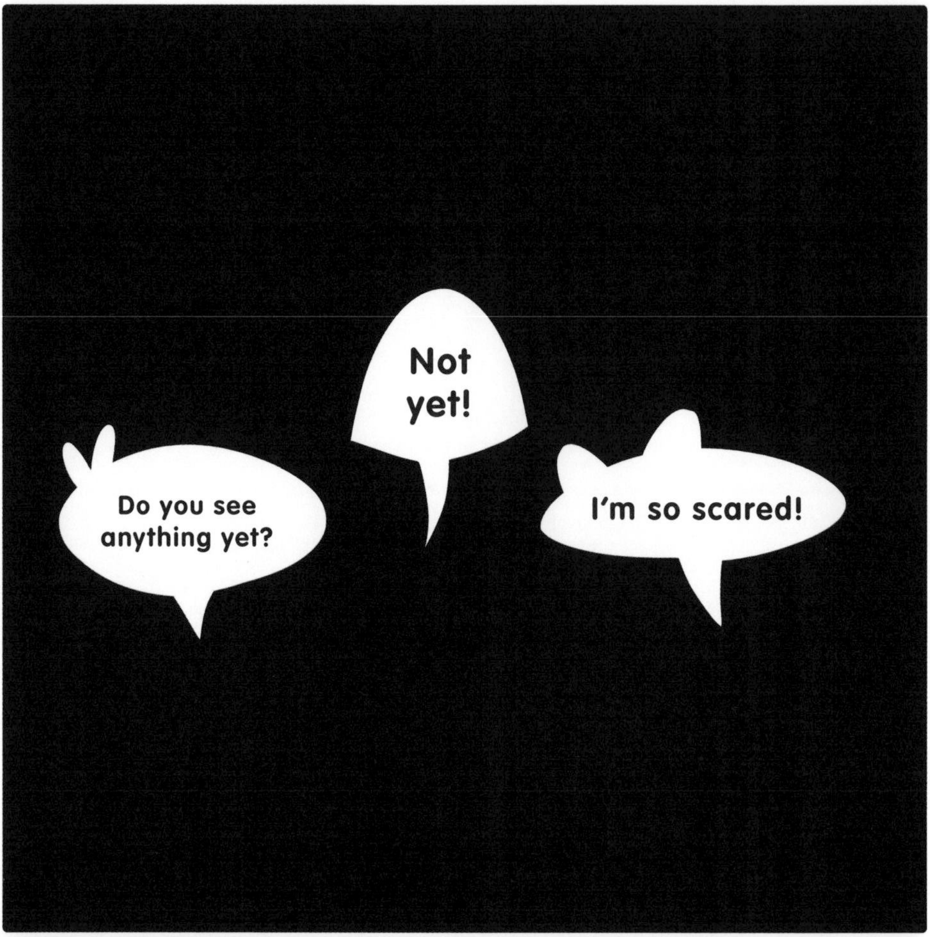
Do you see anything yet?
Not yet!
I'm so scared!

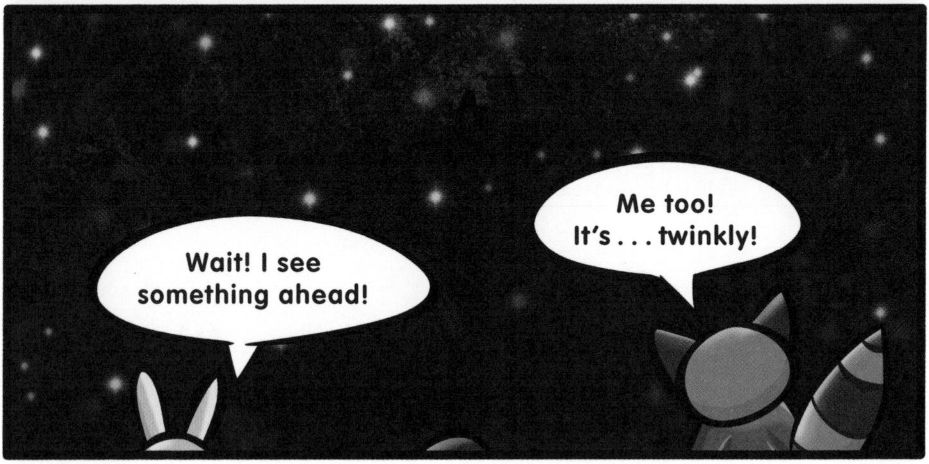
Wait! I see something ahead!
Me too! It's . . . twinkly!

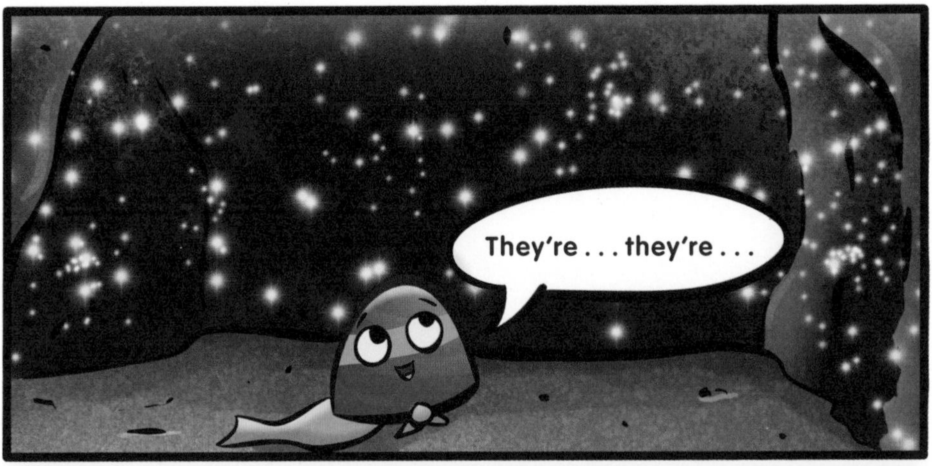
They're . . . they're . . .

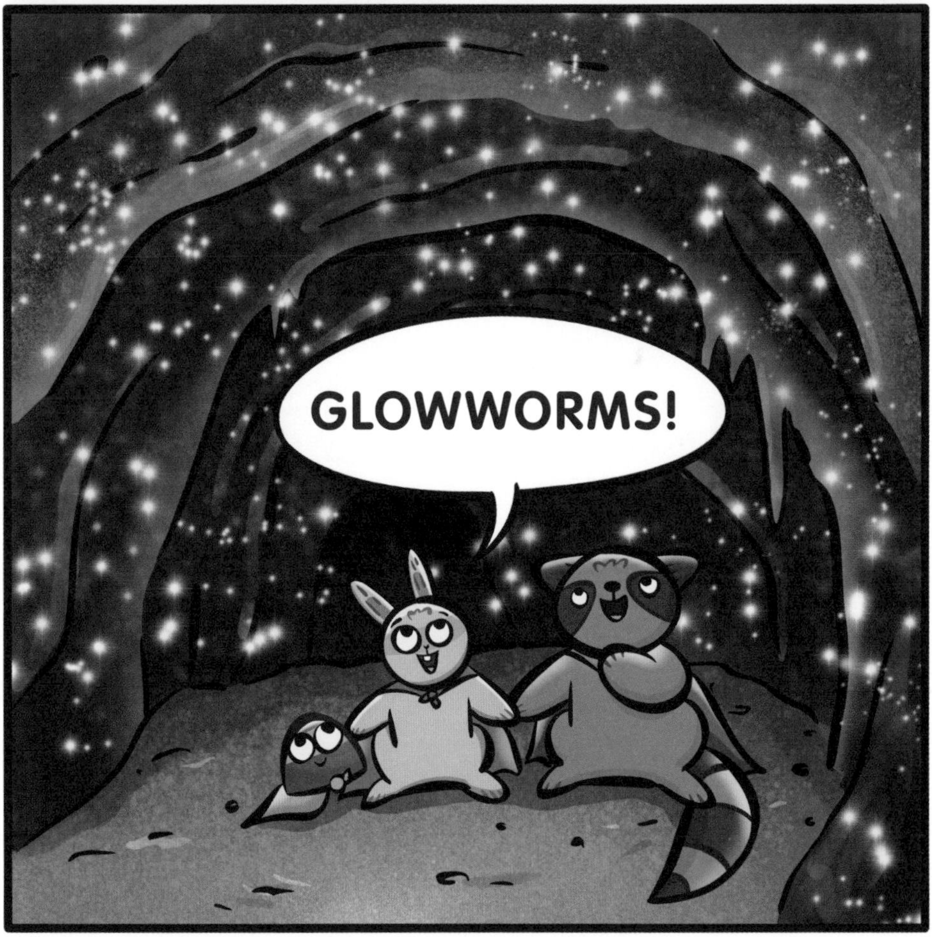
GLOWWORMS!

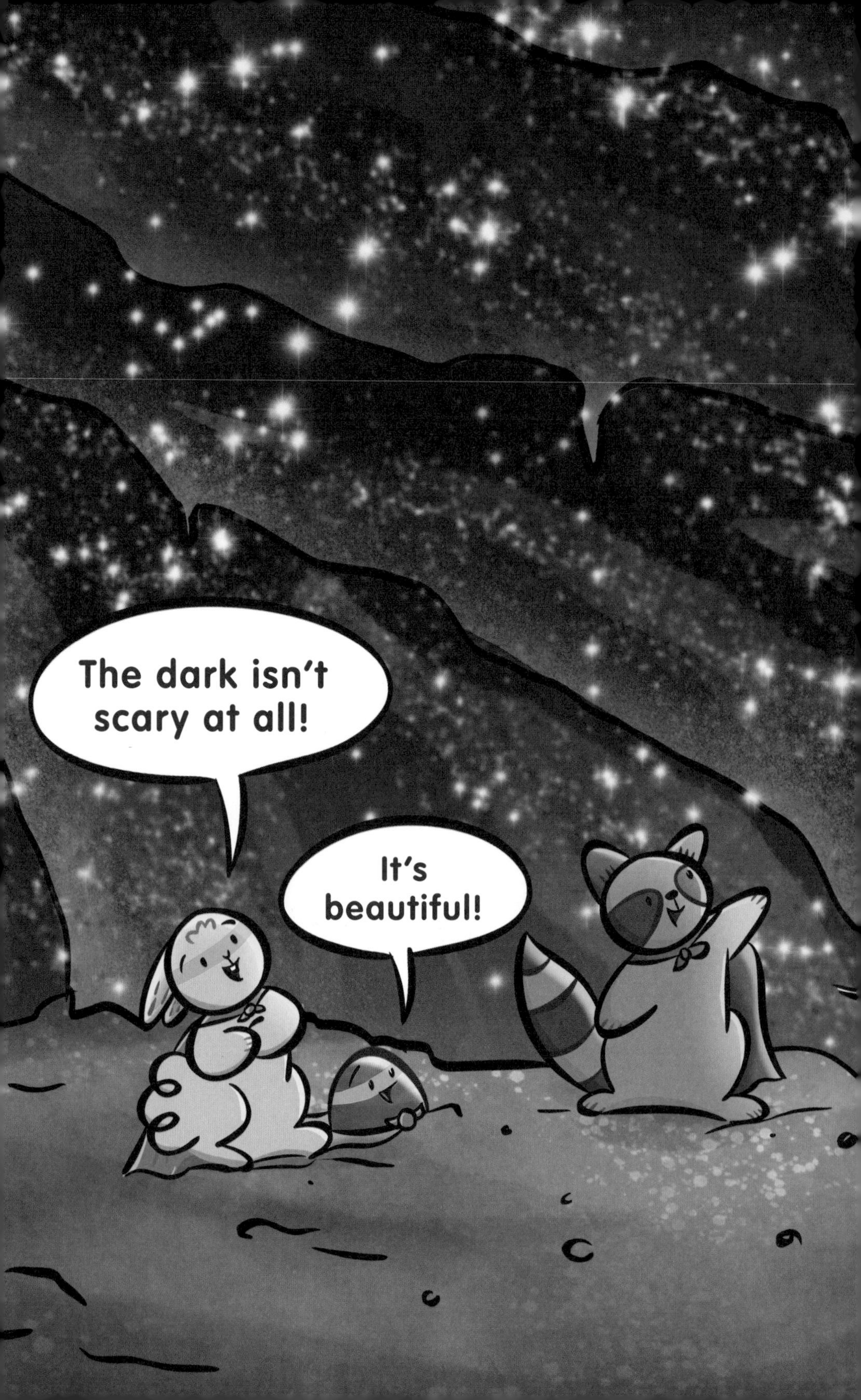
The dark isn't scary at all!
It's beautiful!

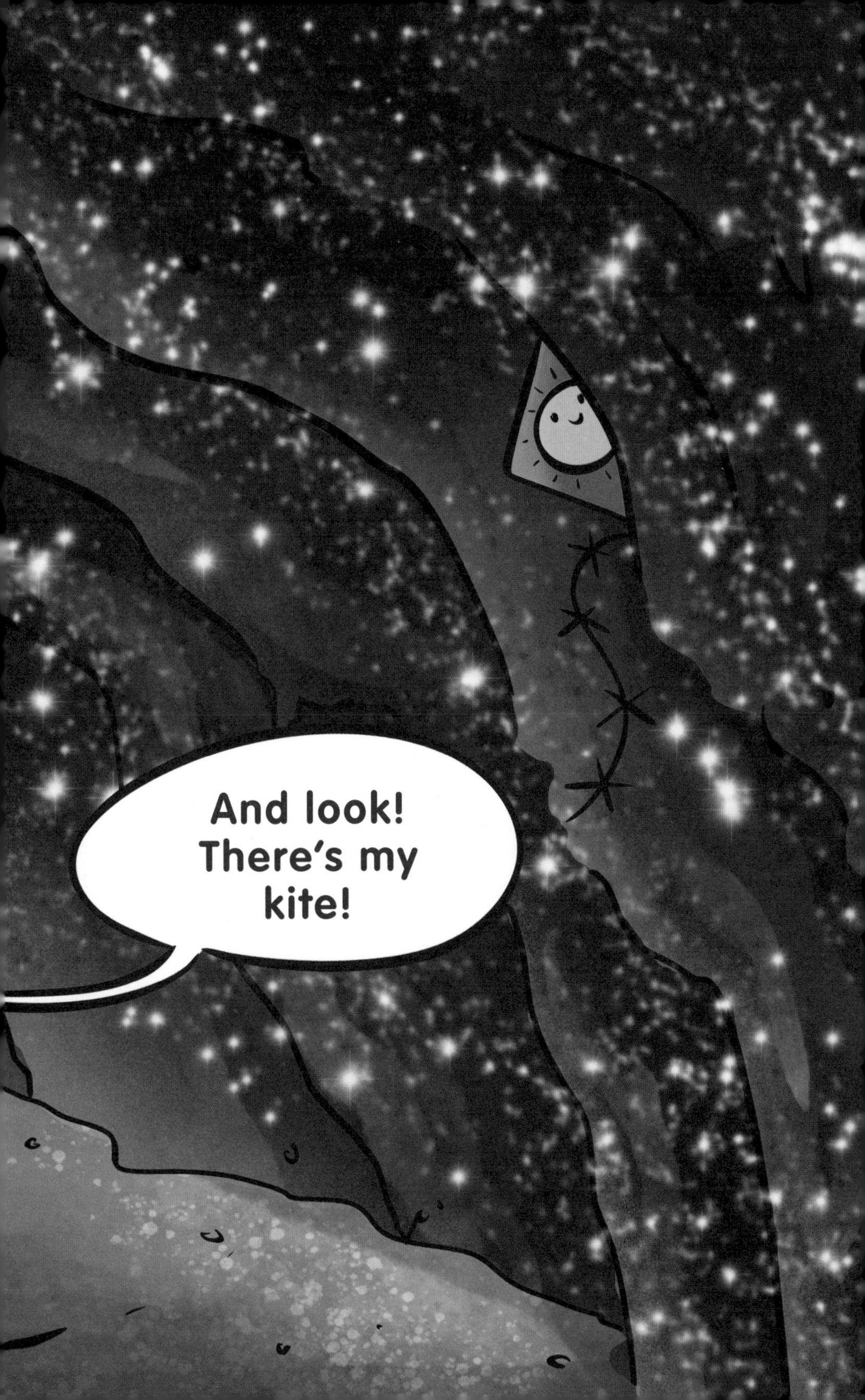
And look! There's my kite!

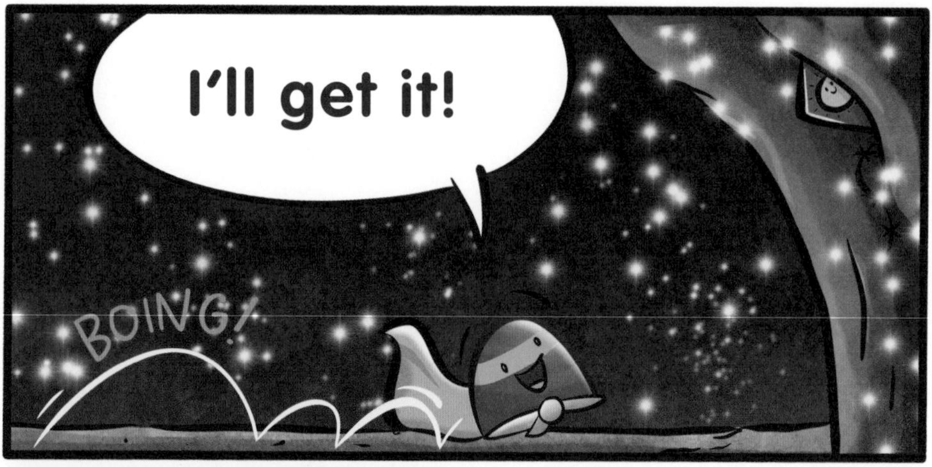
I'll get it!
BOING!

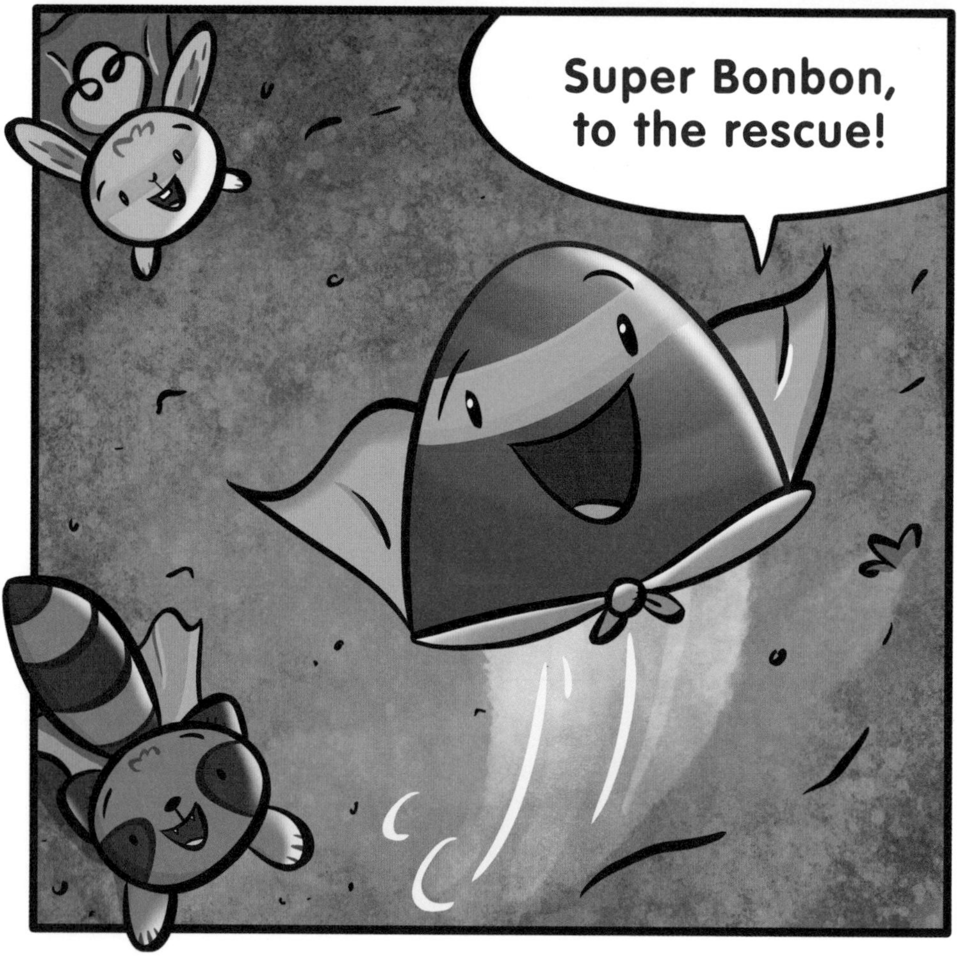
Super Bonbon,
to the rescue!

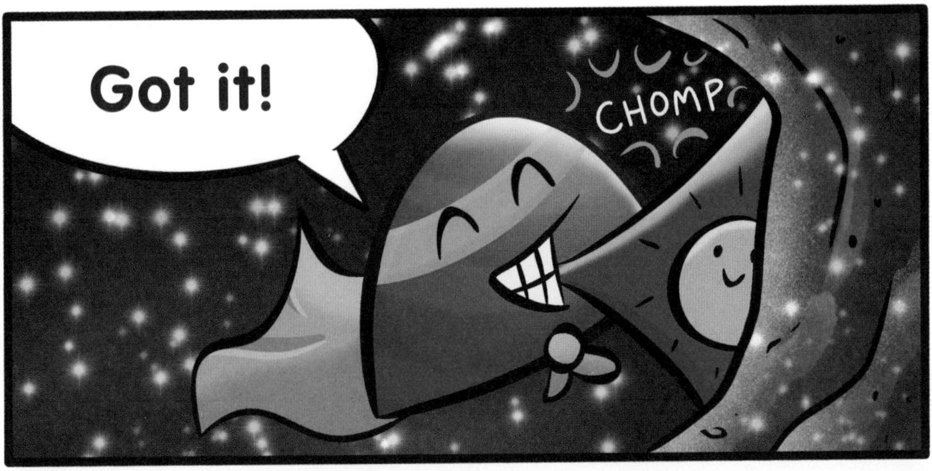
Got it!
CHOMP

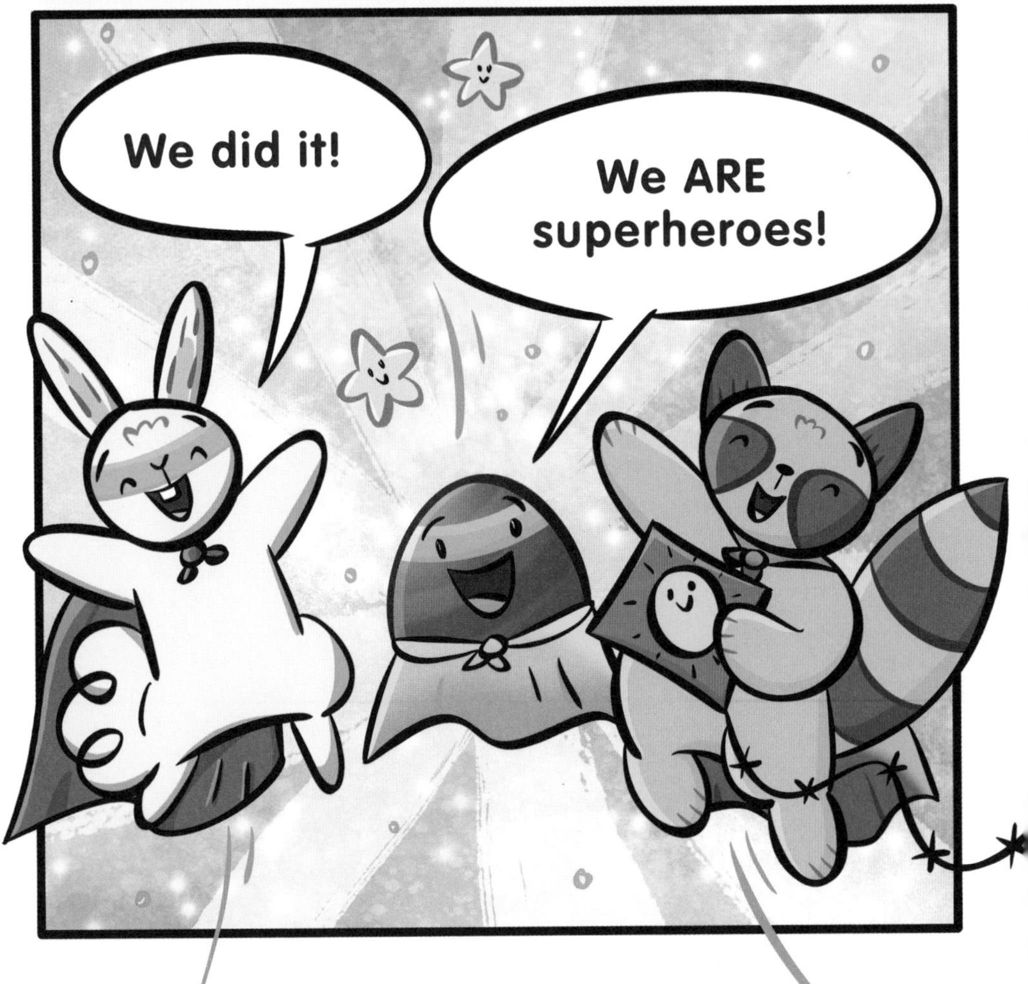
We did it!
We ARE superheroes!

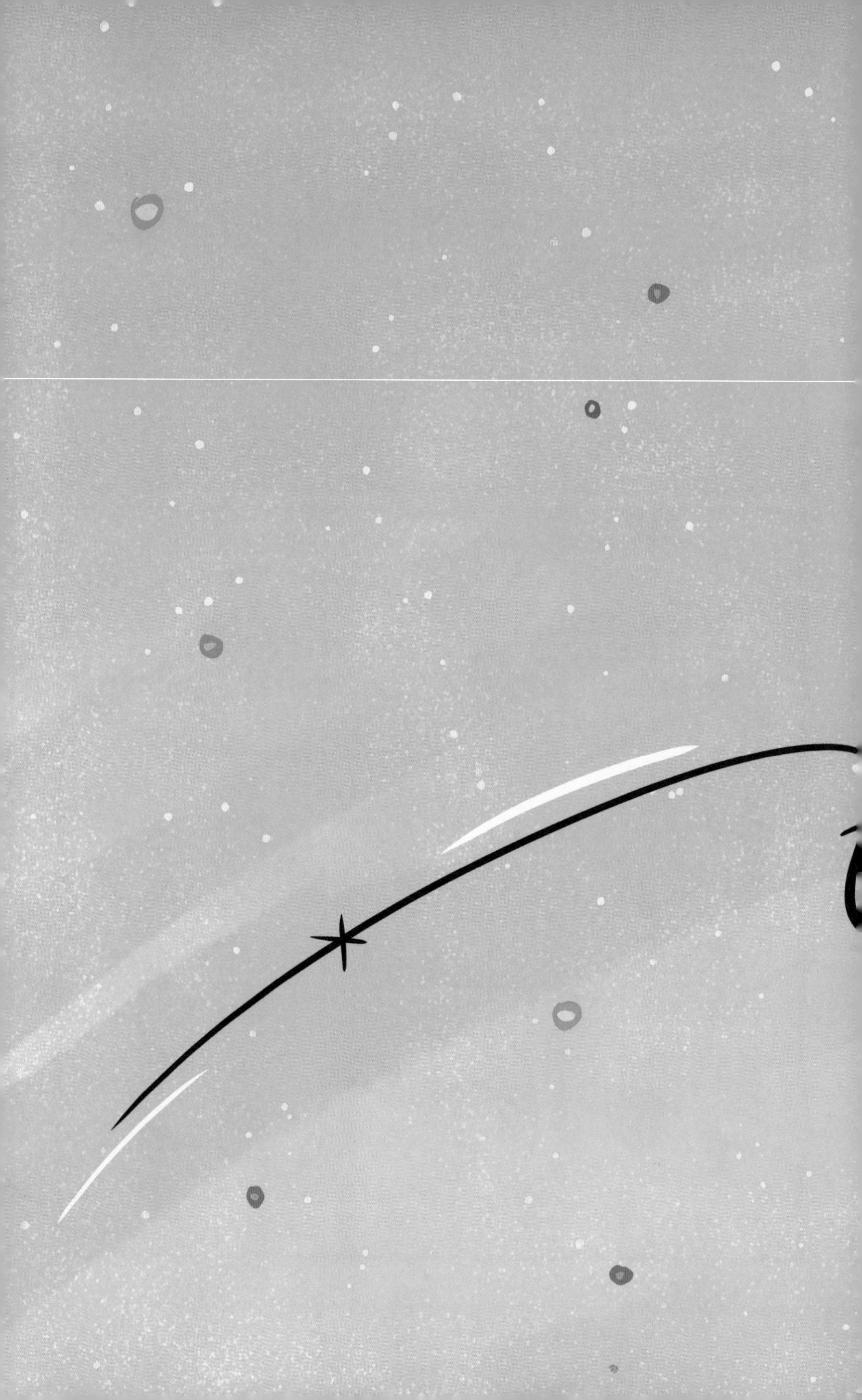

A
SUPERHERO
PICNIC

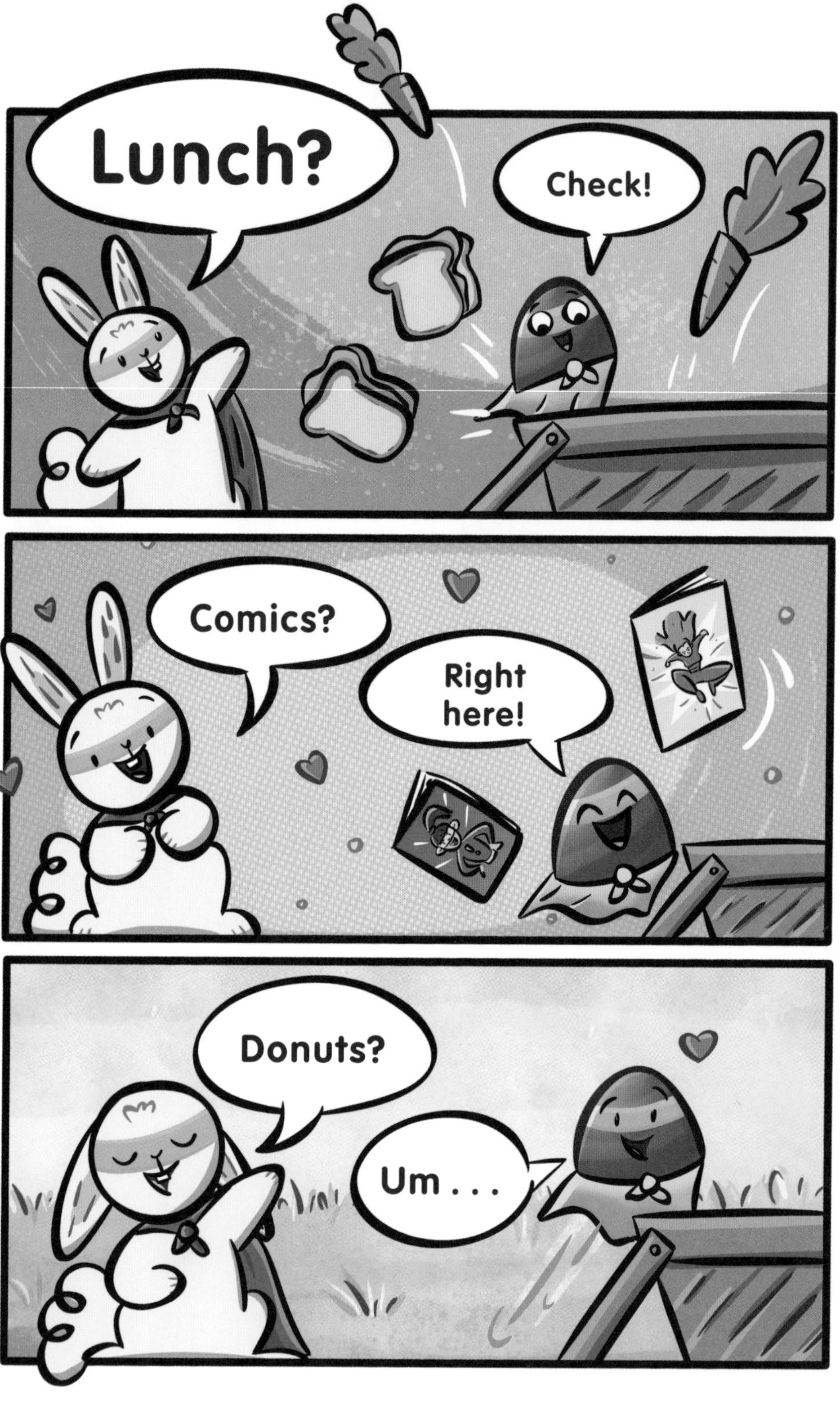
Lunch?
Check!
Comics?
Right here!
Donuts?
Um . . .

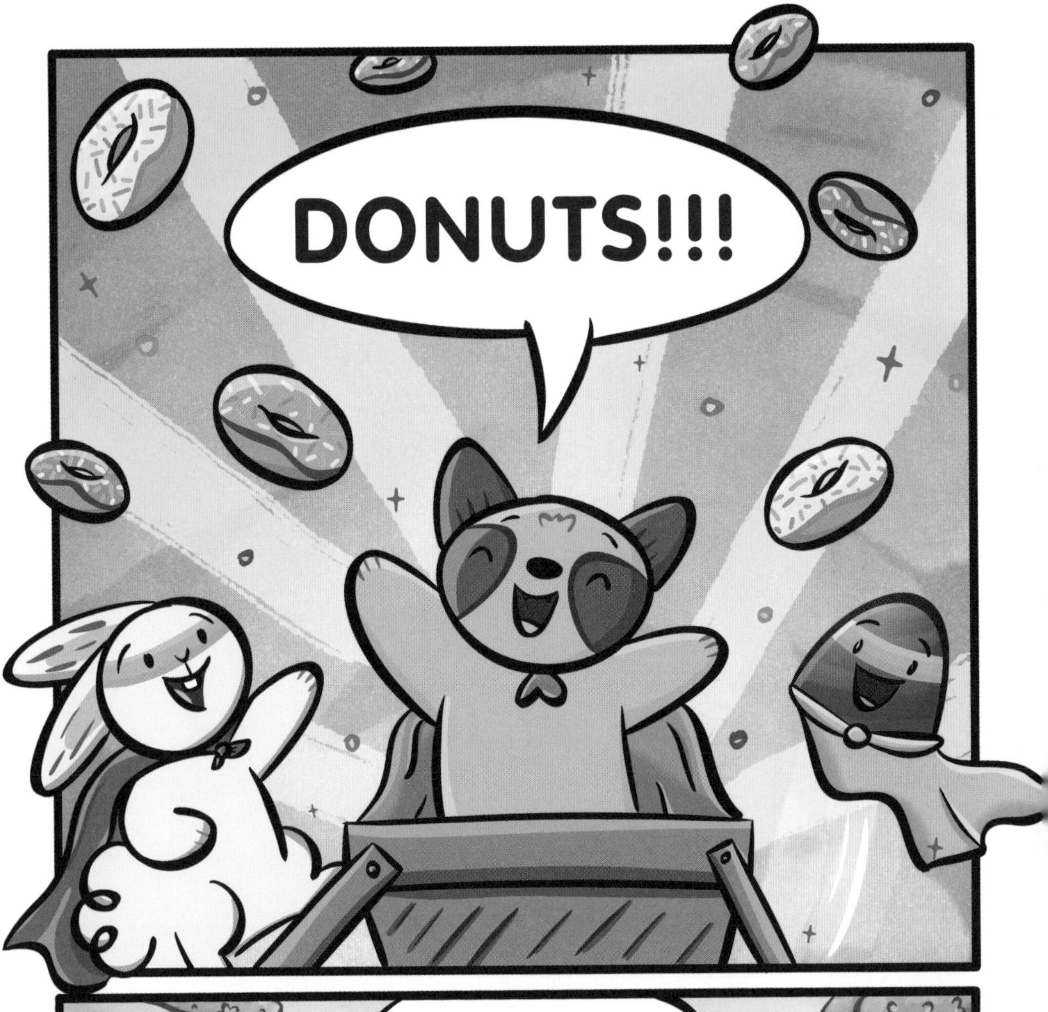
DONUTS!!!

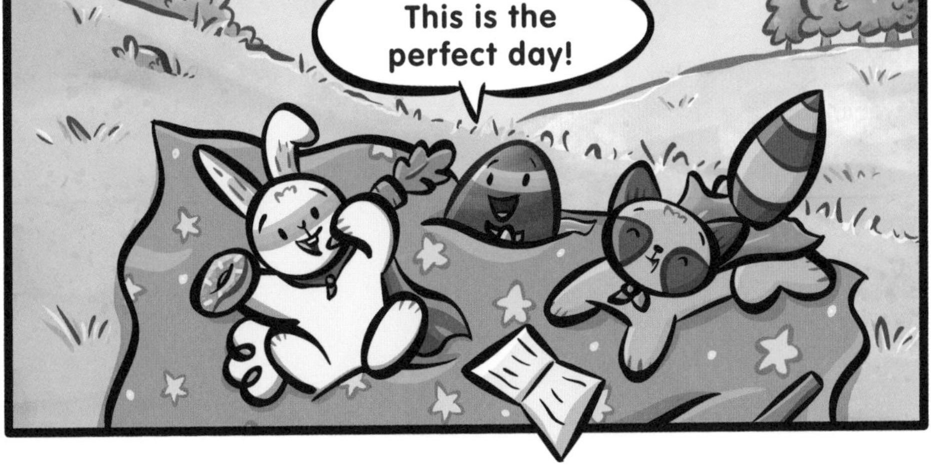
This is the perfect day!

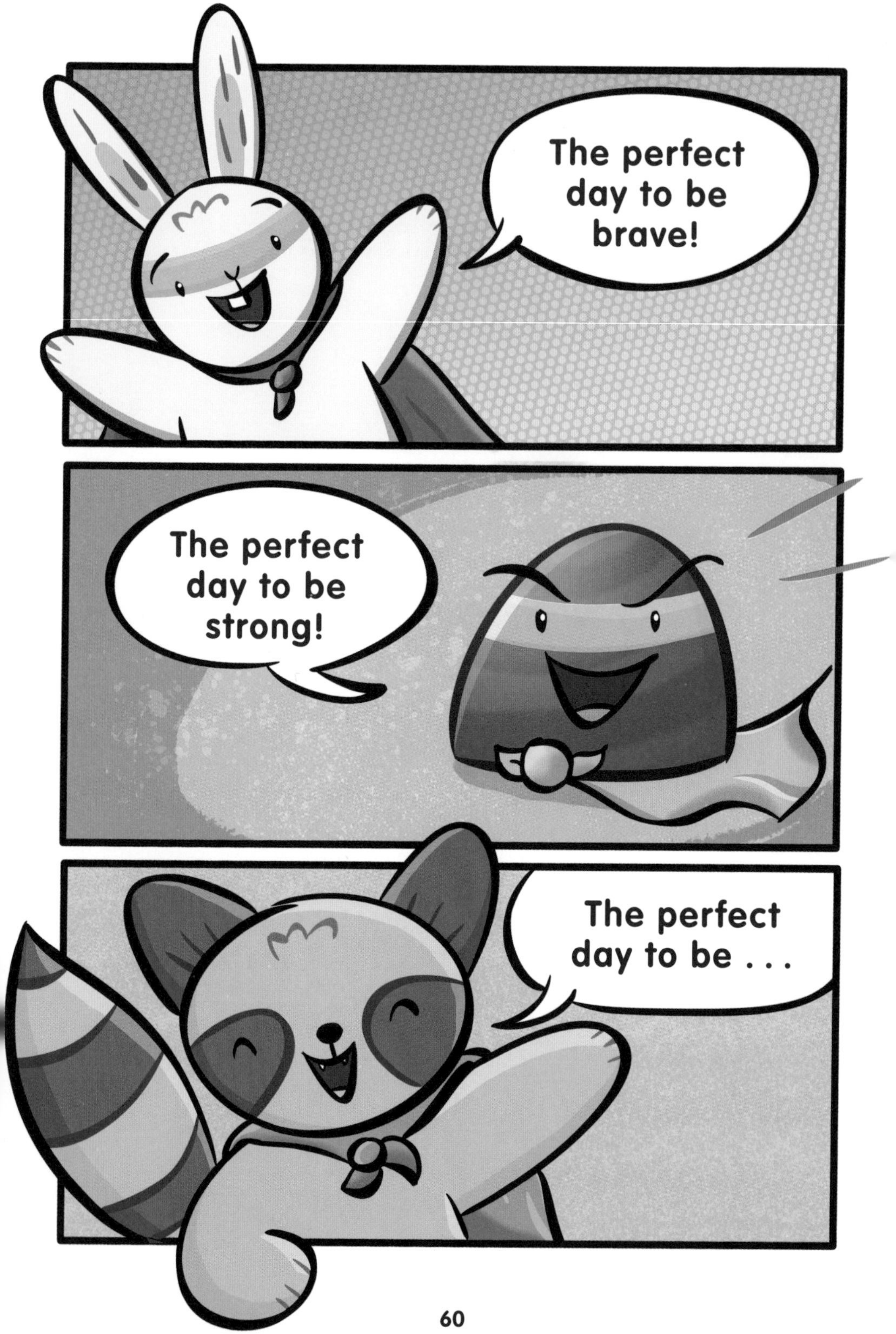
The perfect day to be brave!
The perfect day to be strong!
The perfect day to be . . .

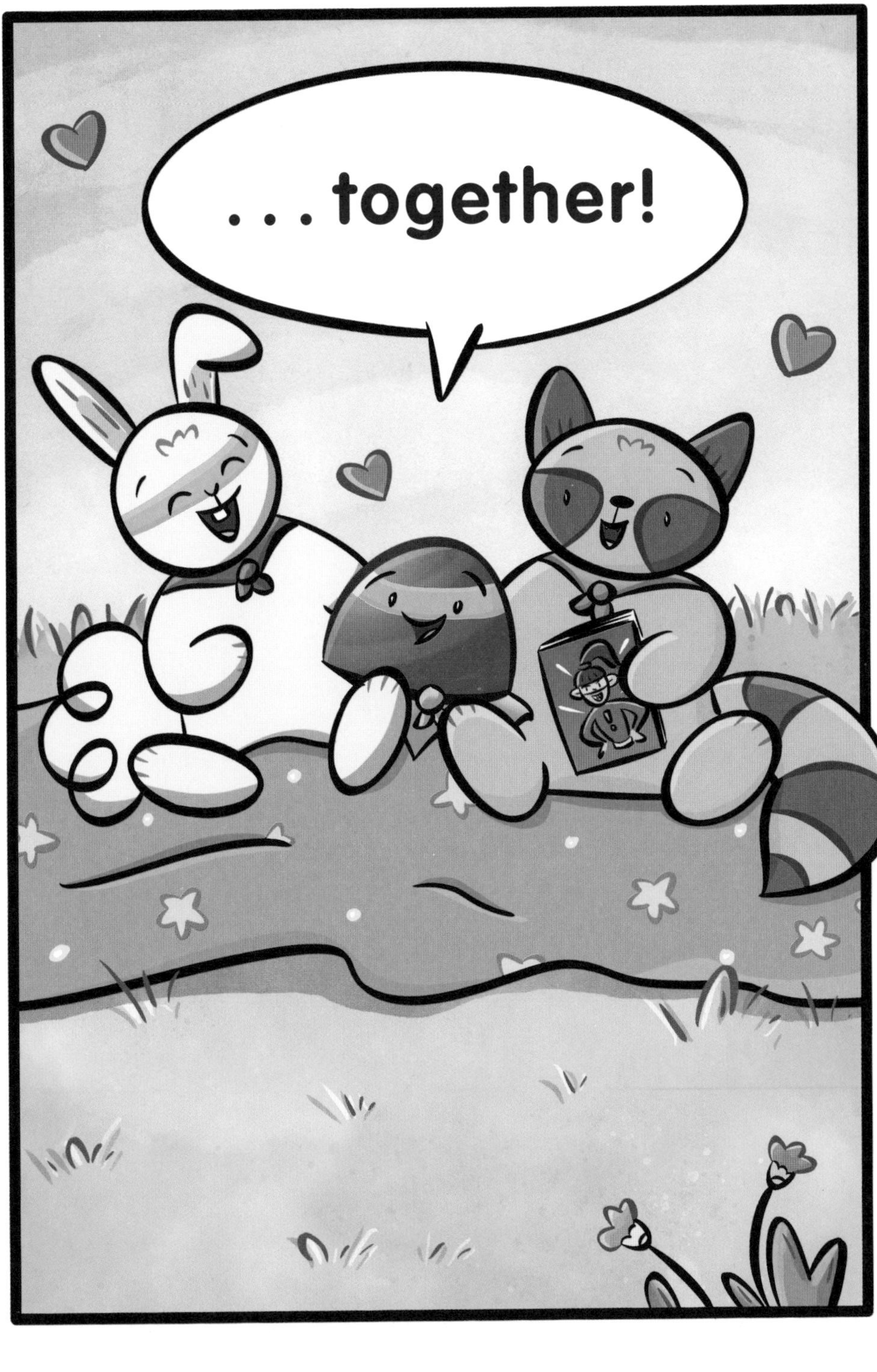
. . . together!

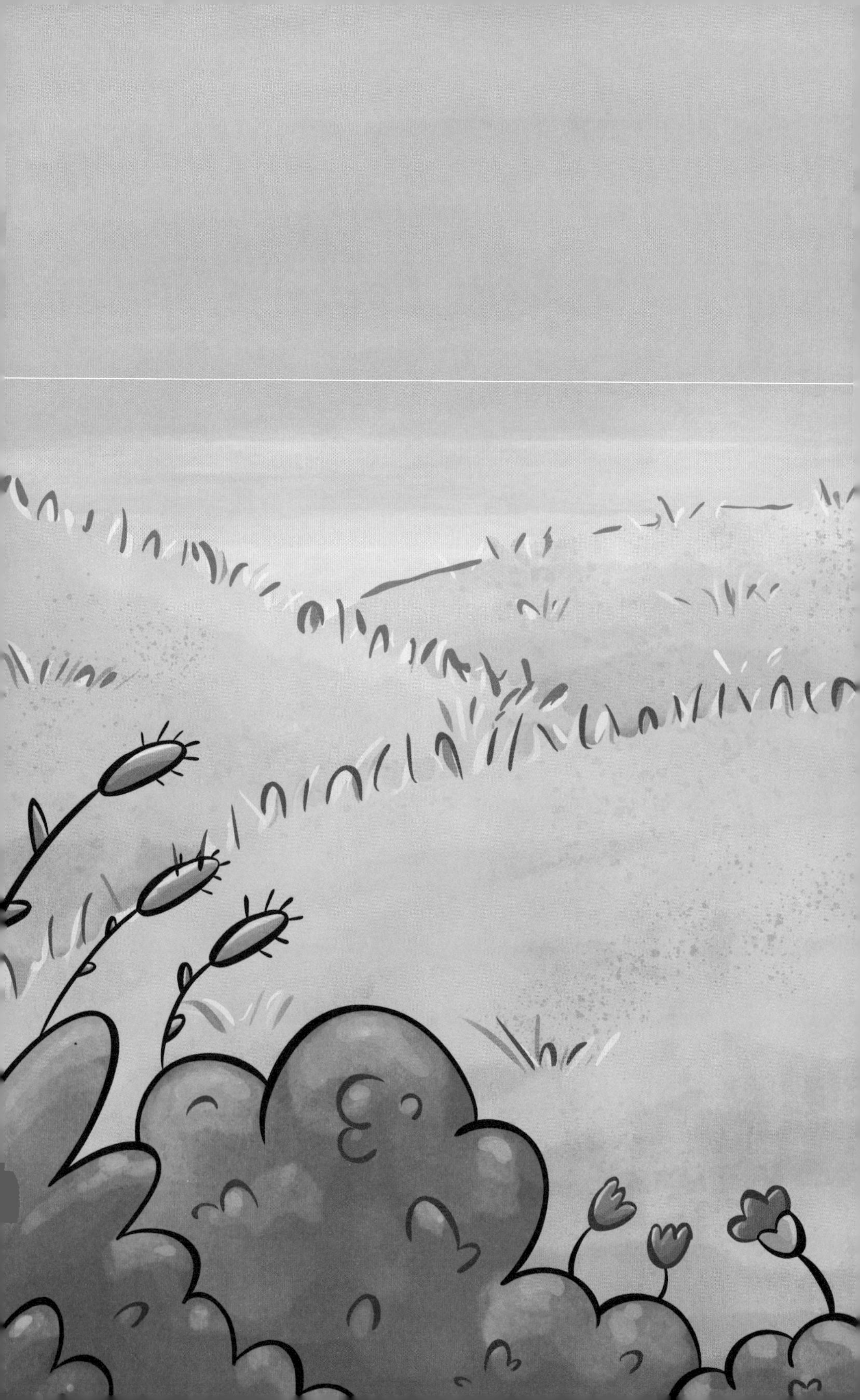

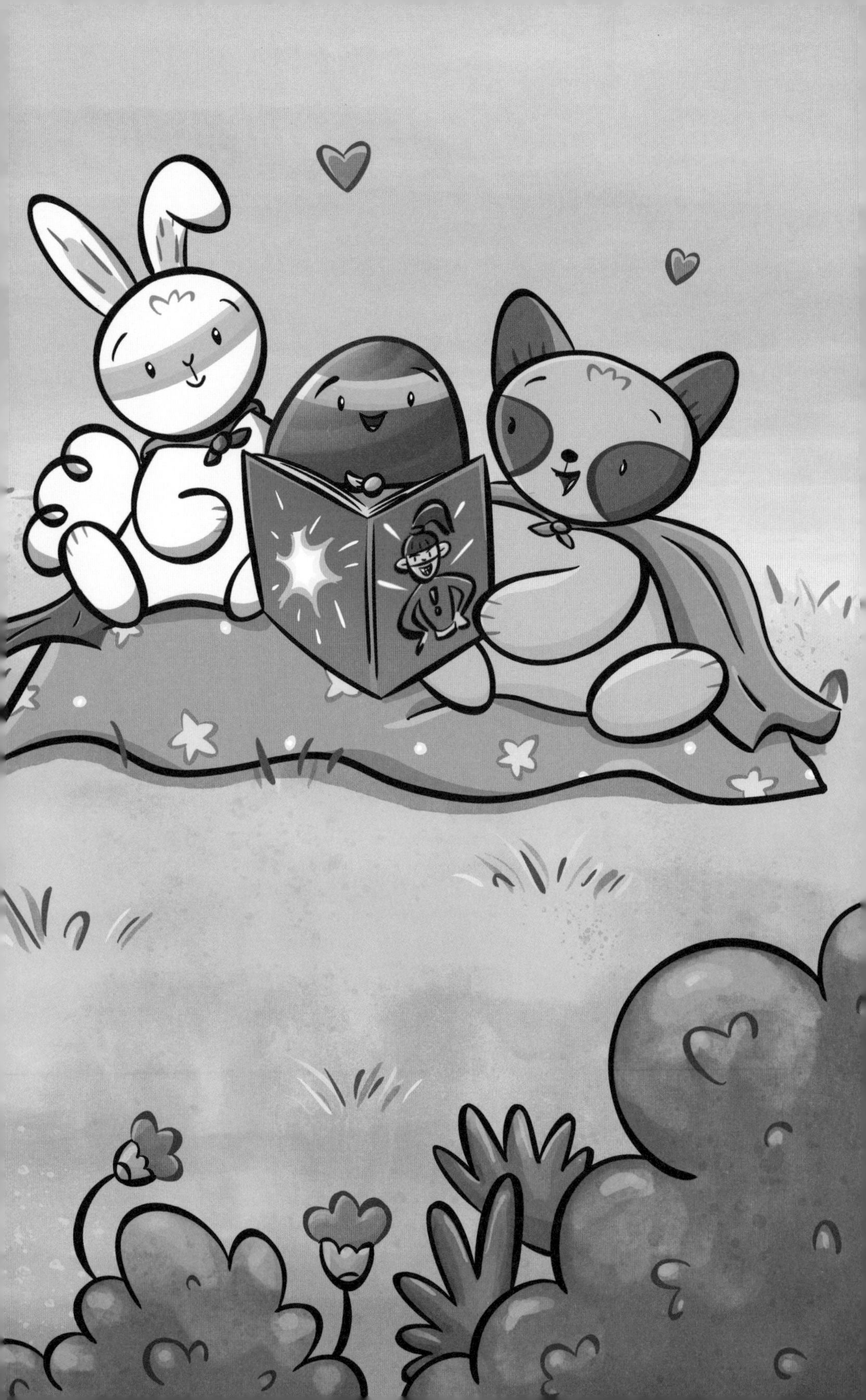

JESS KEATING is an award-winning author, cartoonist, zoologist, and creative coach. She is the creator of over a dozen fiction and nonfiction books, including *Eat Your Rocks, Croc!*; *Set Your Alarm, Sloth!*; and the Elements of Genius middle-grade series. She lives in Ontario, Canada, where she's surrounded by books, bunnies, and bonbons. To learn more, tweet her @Jess_Keating or visit jesskeatingbooks.com, where she shares classes and resources for creative living.